MARINE'S PROMISE

IRON HORSE LEGACY BOOK #3

ELLE JAMES

TWISTED PAGE INC

MARINE'S PROMISE

IRON HORSE LEGACY BOOK #2

New York Times & *USA Today*
Bestselling Author

ELLE JAMES

EBOOK ISBN: 978-1-62695-267-6

PRINT ISBN: 978-1-62695-268-3

Dedicated to my father. I miss him so very much. A good, kind man who taught me so much in his own quiet way.
Elle James

AUTHOR'S NOTE

Enjoy other military books by Elle James
Brotherhood Protectors Series
Montana SEAL (#1)
Bride Protector SEAL (#2)
Montana D-Force (#3)
Cowboy D-Force (#4)
Montana Ranger (#5)
Montana Dog Soldier (#6)
Montana SEAL Daddy (#7)
Montana Ranger's Wedding Vow (#8)
Montana SEAL Undercover Daddy (#9)
Cape Cod SEAL Rescue (#10)
Montana SEAL Friendly Fire (#11)
Montana SEAL's Mail-Order Bride (#12)
Montana Rescue
Hot SEAL, Salty Dog

Visit ellejames.com for more titles and release dates
For hot cowboys, visit her alter ego Myla Jackson at
mylajackson.com
and join Elle James Newsletter at http://
ellejames.com/ElleContact.htm

CHAPTER 1

EMILY TREMONT STEPPED out of the law offices of Halston, Butler & Kenner Attorneys at Law and drew in a deep breath of the cool Montana air. The wind tugged at the hem of her skirt, wrapping it around her thighs, making her wish she'd worn a thicker pair of tights underneath it.

Already, summer had shifted into fall, and leaves were changing colors. Before long, the jet stream would dip low and whip the leaves from their branches.

She clutched the legal-sized envelope close to her chest and hurried toward her SUV.

Emily slipped into the driver's seat and winced as dull pain shot through her hip, reminding her it had only been three months since the car crash. Three months since she'd lost her husband. Three months since she'd lost the baby she'd been carrying. During that three months, she'd had surgery and spent much of her time in physical therapy, re-learning how to walk on her new hip. Her focus and determination to recover had been fueled by the need to know the truth.

Who had shot her husband?

That one shot had killed her husband, while he'd been driving sixty miles an hour down a country highway. She might not have been so adamant to find the killer if her husband had been the only victim. But she'd been pregnant with their first child, and in the car when he'd been shot.

The resulting wreck had completely changed her life. All she could remember from that night was the smack of the bullet against the windshield, Alex's blood and brain matter splattering across her face, and the rush of rocks, boulders and trees coming at them as they'd plunged over the side of the road and down a hill into a ravine.

Thankfully, the impact had rendered her unconscious. When she'd woken briefly to the blur of lights in a hospital hallway, pain had knifed through her head, hip and belly. The pain had been so intense, she'd passed out.

The next time she'd opened her eyes, her sister stood beside her hospital bed staring down at her, a worried frown pressing her eyebrows together. She'd taken Emily's hand in hers. "Hey," she'd said.

"Hey," Emily had replied. Her voice came out as a croak. "What happened?"

2

Her sister's frown deepened. "Don't you remember?"

"Remember what?" Emily squinted, as if by concentrating hard she could pull memories out of her cloudy brain.

"You know...," her sister murmured, "the accident."

Emily had stared at her sister in a fog of confusion.

Brenna had raised Emily's hand to her cheek. "I'm sorry."

"Sorry for what?" The fog of her thoughts couldn't latch onto much, especially when her sister wasn't making sense.

"About Alex..." Brenna's lips pressed together, and tears welled in her eyes. "He didn't make it."

Emily stared at her sister, her heart slamming into her ribs. "What do you mean, he didn't make it?"

"Emily, Alex is dead," her sister said.

That had been the first blow.

"And Emily..." her sister's grip tightened on her hand, "you lost the baby."

The resulting rush of emotion had hit her like a tsunami and dragged her back to the abyss of unconsciousness.

Three months had passed since the wreck. During those months, she'd fought through the pain, both physical and emotional, searching for her new normal. Only she still hadn't figured out what normal was.

She pulled the seatbelt around her and clicked it into the buckle. Shifting into reverse, she glanced into her rearview mirror.

A dark SUV sat in the parking space immediately behind where she was parked. Though the windows were tinted, she could see the silhouette of a large man sitting behind the wheel.

Call her paranoid, but after having been in the same vehicle with her husband when he'd been shot, she had good reason to be suspicious.

With the envelope sitting on the seat beside her, she backed out of the parking space and pulled out of the lot onto the main road.

The attorney had given her the package, stating that her husband had left strict instructions that she should receive the package on the third month following his death.

Her hands curled tightly around the steering wheel.

Why would Alex have planned to send her a package three months after his death?

The only reason he would do such a thing would be if he knew there would be somebody coming after him. Perhaps, someone who would want to kill him. He had no other reason to ask for a posthumous delivery.

As far as Emily had known, Alex had been in good health. He hadn't had cancer or a debilitating disease, but he had been acting strangely and secretively over the last year of his life. So much so, Emily had worried Alex had been cheating on her. Their marriage had been rocky at best before he'd become so secretive.

They'd been together since high school. During that ten years, she'd led a guilty life, wondering if she'd chosen the wrong man to marry. In high school, it had been the three of them. Her, Alex and Colin.

They'd been the Three Musketeers, doing everything together, including horseback riding, canoeing, swimming and hiking in the Crazy Mountains. They'd even gone to the prom together, rather than leave one of them without a date.

Emily had had a tough time deciding between the two of them. Ultimately, Colin had made that decision for her when he'd come to her to tell her that he was joining the Marines. He'd known how she'd felt about the military, and she'd thought he'd known how she'd felt about him.

As a teenager, she'd lost her father to the war in Iraq. She hadn't wanted to invest her emotions and her love in someone who would purposely put himself in harm's way, forsaking his loved ones.

Right after high school, Alex had asked her to marry him, and Emily had accepted. Colin had joined the Marines. Thus, their stint as the Three Musketeers had ended.

Colin had returned long enough to attend their wedding. At their simple ceremony, he'd made a promise to Emily that if anything should ever happen to Alex, she could count on Colin to help her in any way.

After Alex's death, Emily figured she was a big girl. She'd made her choice in Alex, and now had to make it on her own.

Colin had his life in the Marines. She didn't even know where in the world he was at the time of Alex's death. Besides, he might also have his own life and be married with a family of his own. The thought had hit her square in the gut and made her own grief deepen.

Hell, after ten years, Colin might not even remember her.

Emily glanced in the rearview mirror.

The SUV that had been behind her in the parking lot, now followed her. This had not been the first time she'd been followed by someone in a dark SUV.

Familiar unease raised gooseflesh on her skin. At the next light, she waited until the light turned green, and then abruptly made a righthand turn. Pressing hard on the accelerator, she sped forward to the next street and turned left.

Another glance in the mirror, affirmed the fact that the SUV was still behind her.

Her gut clenched, and her pulse quickened. At the next corner, she made another sharp right and slammed her foot to the pedal. She sped down the street to the next corner where she could only turn left. She looked back. No headlights shone behind her, but she didn't trust that she'd lost her tail.

Emily took the turn and continued down the lane, emerging onto another street. Before she could react, the dark SUV zoomed out of nowhere and skidded to a halt in front of her, blocking her path.

Emily screamed and slammed on her brakes.

The passenger door of the SUV opened and a large man wearing a ski mask stepped out.

Fear ripped through Emily. She shoved the gear shift into reverse and punched the accelerator with her foot.

Craning her neck to look over her shoulder, she backed down the street she'd just driven on as fast as she could, zigzagging a little as she went.

She shot a glance in front of her and saw that the SUV had turned onto the street and was following her again.

Emily pulled on the steering wheel and spun the vehicle in a 180-degree turn. Then she hit the gas pedal and tried to put as much distance as she could between her and the vehicle behind her.

Another dark SUV pulled out in front of her, blocking the street and her escape.

Refusing to be trapped between the SUV behind her and the one stopped in front of her, Emily jerked the steering wheel, bumped up on the curb, swerved around a giant oak tree, drove across a yard, missed a mailbox and bumped back onto the road on the other side of the SUV.

Driving faster than she'd ever driven before, Emily raced away from the two SUVs that had tried to trap her. She had to get to someplace safe. Someplace well-lit, with lots of people. And soon.

The sun had tipped well below the horizon, casting the land, trees and houses into shadow.

Rather than head toward Eagle Rock where she lived, Emily remained in Bozeman, determined to find a place with a lot of people. She needed to hide in a crowd until the people pursuing her gave up.

Most of the small businesses had closed for the night. Their windows were dark, their staffs had long since gone home. Two sets of headlights fell in behind her, speeding toward her, quickly closing the distance between them.

Desperate to find help, Emily turned again toward the center of Bozeman. In front of her, a lot of cars were gathered around what appeared to be a tavern. A light shone down on the entrance.

Emily aimed her vehicle at the building. At the last second, she turned the vehicle sharply to the right and slammed on the brakes. The SUV slid sideways, coming to a screeching halt in front of the door.

Shifting into park, she grabbed the package from the front seat, shoved it into her purse and looped the strap over her shoulder. Taking a deep breath, she pushed open her door, dropped out, ducked and made a dash for the tavern, careful to keep her head and body lower than the top of her vehicle.

The two dark SUVs barreled toward her SUV without slowing.

Emily ran for the entrance and threw herself inside, praying her pursuers didn't follow.

But they did.

COLIN MCKINNON HAD SPENT most of the day combing through Bozeman, searching for a girl with a unicorn tattoo on her wrist. He was convinced the woman knew something about his father's disappearance. Perhaps she held a clue as to where they could find him. His entire family had been searching now for two weeks, praying for a sign that he was still alive.

Missing since the day he and a posse of men had set out to find an escaped con, John McKinnon hadn't turned up. No sign, no clues, until now, and no body. A fact that maintained a glimmer of hope to the family.

None of his children could imagine him dead. The man was larger than life, tough and fair. He couldn't be dead. Thus, the reason for the return of the McKinnon siblings to the Iron Horse Ranch. They'd come home to join the search for the patriarch of their family.

For the past two weeks, they'd combed the woods and mountains where the older McKinnon had last been seen. A snowstorm and an avalanche had buried any traces or tracks.

Their first clue came when they'd found John McKinnon's ring on Beau Faulkner's finger. They'd immediately jumped to the conclusion that Beau had been behind his father's disappearance. But Beau had insisted he'd purchased the ring from a pawn shop in Bozeman.

The pawn shop owner had said he'd gotten it from a bleached-blond woman with a unicorn tattoo on her wrist. She hadn't left her name or a forwarding address. Colin had left his phone number with the man, asking him to call if the woman came back.

Although it was like searching for a needle in a haystack the size of a state, Colin hadn't given up hope. Thus, his reason for being in Bozeman, an hour away from the family ranch near Eagle Rock, Montana. He'd spent the entire day going from tattoo parlor to tattoo parlor, asking if any of the artists had tattooed a unicorn on the wrist of a blonde.

Not one of the tattoo parlors had panned out. Tired and disheartened, Colin had ducked into the Big Sky Tavern, a place he frequented on his rare visits to Bozeman, hoping someone had seen the woman with the unicorn tattoo. And if he didn't find her, at least he could have a beer and something to eat before he headed back to Eagle Rock.

He glanced around the tavern. Busy for a week-night, the tables were all taken. Unwilling to wait for one to be vacated, he settled on a stool at the corner of the bar nearest to the entrance and ordered a draft beer.

After the bartender delivered his drink, he sat

back, lifted his mug to his lips and took a long satisfying swallow of the cool liquid.

He'd just set his mug on the counter when a woman burst through the front door, running full speed and plowed into him.

No sooner had she had slammed into his chest then the entire wall of the tavern, door and all, came crashing toward him.

He grabbed the woman and flung her and himself out of the way of snapping timbers and flying debris.

Tavern patrons screamed and ran for the back of the building as the shiny body of a vehicle slid sideways through the wall, coming to a stop inches from the bar where Colin had been enjoying his beer moments before.

When the vehicle and the wall stopped moving, Colin pushed the woman in his embrace to arm's length. "Are you okay?"

She nodded and turned her face up to him, a frown wrinkling her familiar brow. "Colin?"

Recognition dawned on him, and his hands tightened on her arms. "Emily. Holy hell. What just happened?"

She shot a glance through the dust at the destroyed wall, her eyes wide. "They didn't stop." She shook her head and met his gaze. "I don't think I'm safe here. Heck, I don't think anyone is safe as long as I'm here." She looked around at the customers standing near the rear of the tavern.

Men and women held their children close. A lady

was crying softly, and the bartender had his cell-phone pressed to his ear, calling 911.

"I need to leave," Emily said. "Now." She stepped back, out of his arms and chewed on her bottom lip. "But that's my car. I don't have a way home."

"I can get you there," Colin said. "But first tell me why your vehicle is parked inside the tavern."

She laughed, the sound a bit on the hysterical side. "You think I put it there?" She snorted. "My bet is that one of the two SUVs that've been following me hit it, pushing it into the wall."

"Why would someone do that?" Colin asked.

Emily threw up her hands. "The hell if I know. One minute I'm leaving my attorney's office, the next minute, I'm being followed, almost trapped and chased by a couple of SUVs. You tell me what that's all about. Hell if I know." She looked around, her gaze going to the rear of the building. "All I know is that we should get out of here before they come back or the walls cave in."

"We'll go out the back door. But I'm sure the sheriff will want to question you about the people who did this to you." He cupped her elbow and hustled her to the back exit and out into the night. The tavern patrons left the building and moved around to the front where they stood in a semi-circle around Emily's mangled vehicle, talking in hushed voices and pointing at the damage to the SUV and the building.

A siren wailed from a couple blocks away. Soon, a

sheriff's vehicle arrived with blazing lights. Another one joined the first, along with an ambulance and a fire engine.

The emergency medical technicians went to work helping those injured by flying debris.

An imposing man in uniform stepped out of a county sheriff's vehicle, a frown creasing his forehead. "Someone want to tell me what the Sam-hill happened here?"

"And you are?"

"Sheriff Mizner." He held out his hand.

"Colin McKinnon. And this is Emily Tremont." Colin stepped forward with Emily in the crook of his arm and shook the sheriff's hand. "Sheriff, apparently, there's been a hit and run."

The sheriff pulled a pad and pen from his pocket and made notes as Colin and Emily filled him in on what they knew.

"Any idea why these people in the SUVs would want to hurt you?" the lawman asked.

Emily shook her head. "I have no idea. But it's not the first time I've been followed. It's been happening over the past three months. Only, this is the first time they've attacked."

Colin leaned back, his frown deepening. "You've been followed for three months?"

She shrugged. "I think so. I didn't realize it was happening for the first couple of weeks following Alex's death, but when they continued to follow, it became obvious." She twisted her fingers around the strap of her purse. "They've had me so spooked, I had an alarm system installed in my house." She stared out at the darkness. "Why they decided to attack me now, I don't know."

The sheriff touched her arm. "Ms. Tremont, why didn't you let us know? At the very least, you should have notified your county sheriff's department."

She shrugged. "I wasn't sure it was a problem, until tonight. Besides, you and Sheriff Barron over in Eagle Rock have had enough on your plates, what with John McKinnon's disappearance."

Colin's gut clenched at the mention of his father. The man had been missing now for a couple weeks with only a single vague clue to go on. The woman with the unicorn tattoo.

The sheriff shook his head. "Your safety is just as important as us finding McKinnon." He met Colin's gaze.

Colin nodded. "That's right." He turned to Emily. "Did you get a look at their license plates?"

Emily shook her head. "No. It was dark, and I was too busy trying to avoid being caught by them." Her brow twisted, and she faced the sheriff. "Do you think they could be the same people who killed my husband?"

Sheriff Mizner sighed. "I don't know. I'm sorry to say, we still don't have so much as a single lead on the case. We've been working with Sheriff Barron, since the case crosses counties, and we have a few more resources than he does. We haven't found any evidence that points to the person who shot your husband."

"The state crime lab has had his computer all this time." Emily crossed her arms over her chest. "As much time as he spent working on that computer, you'd think he'd have left some kind of clues. It has to be someone he worked with. Someone whose books he worked on. A client. A client's spouse...someone." Her voice caught on the last word, and her throat worked as she swallowed hard.

Colin had heard about Alex's death. He'd just come off a mission in Syria when he'd gotten the message from his mother. Tagged with going right back out on another taskforce, he hadn't been able to help Emily as he'd promised when she'd married his best friend.

The sheriff touched her arm. "Between my detectives here in Gallatin County and Sheriff Barron's county's resources, we've questioned more than half his clients and haven't found anything to make us suspicious of any one of his contacts." He dropped his hand. "Did he keep a separate database on another computer? A flash drive or data storage device locked up in a safe?"

Emily shook her head. "I don't know. He had his work. I had mine, working real estate. I've looked through his file cabinets, desk and the safe in his office. I didn't find anything I haven't already given you or Sheriff Barron."

"I find it hard to believe his death was a random

shooting," the sheriff said.

"It couldn't have been. And it's been three months." Emily narrowed her eyes at the sheriff. "You'd think by now, you'd have found something."

Sheriff Mizner's lips pressed into a tight line. "We're doing the best we can." One of his deputies called out his name. He raised a hand and gave the man a chin lift before returning his attention to Emily. "Do you want me have Sheriff Barron position a deputy in front of your house 24/7?"

Emily shook her head. "He doesn't have the manpower to do that. I have a gun and a security system. I'll take care of myself."

"If you need anything—" the sheriff started.

"I know how to dial 911." Emily's lips twisted. "And I know you're doing the best you can, given your resources. It's just frustrating and frightening, knowing Alex's killer is still free." She waved her hand toward her ruined vehicle. "And now this."

"We'll see what we can find. Maybe one of the other business owners has a security camera and caught the perps' vehicles so we can get a make and model, and maybe even a license plate." He held out his hand. "Mr. McKinnon, nice to meet you. Rest assured...we're also helping Sheriff Barron and the state police in the search to find your father. Now, if you'll excuse me..." He hurried toward the deputy who'd been waiting patiently for his attention.

Colin was sick to learn that Emily had been the target of a stalker and someone who'd attempted to kill her by smashing into her car. "I should've been here," Colin murmured.

Emily frowned. "It wasn't your problem. Besides, you have a life of your own in the Marine Corps."

Her words weren't sharp or accusing, but they struck Colin in the gut, as they had ten years ago when Emily had agreed to marry Alex. She'd wanted stability, a place to set down roots and a husband who didn't put himself in harm's way.

Alex had been all that. He'd been the safe choice. At least, they'd all thought he was. Until three months ago, when he'd been shot and killed while driving home with his wife.

Since when did accountants generate enough rage to make someone want to kill them? Everyone had loved Alex. He'd been a nice, smart guy who'd loved Emily.

Knowing Alex would be a good, safe choice for Emily, Colin hadn't fought to tear her away from him. Oh, he'd wanted to, but he'd always dreamed of joining the military. And Emily hadn't wanted anything to do with it.

Having lost her father to Operation Enduring Freedom, she couldn't risk her heart to a man who would leave her behind to go into battle.

Colin shook his head. And Alex had been the one to die from a bullet wound. He mourned his friend and hated the situation it had put Emily in, but the irony wasn't lost on him.

"Can I go home now?" Emily asked, staring at her

SUV covered in debris from the wall of the tavern. "I'm tired."

"You bet." Colin slipped an arm around her waist and led her toward his truck, parked at the far end of the parking lot.

Once he handed her up into the passenger seat and helped her secure her seatbelt, he rounded the hood of the pickup and climbed in behind the wheel.

Emily stared forward, her face pale, her expression guarded. "Thank you, Colin. But once you drop me off at my house in Eagle Rock, you don't have to stick around. I can take care of myself. You have to find your father. My problem isn't yours."

Colin paused with his hand on the key, his brow pushing downward. He sat back and stared at her. "I might not have been there for you when Alex died... but I'm here now, and I intend to stay."

Her gaze shot to his. "You can't. You're still in the Marine Corps. They aren't going to let you stay for long."

"I'll stay as long as it takes." He reached out and took her hand in his. "I made a promise, that if anything happened to Alex, I'd look after you."

She tried to tug her hand free, but he refused to release it. "I'm not your problem. You don't have to look after me. My mother taught me not to rely on any man for my support or happiness. I should have listened ten years ago. But I'm listening now." She lifted her chin and stared into his eyes. "All I need from you is a ride back to Eagle Rock. If you can't do that, I'll get one of the sheriff's deputies to transport me there." She stared down at his hand. "Let go of my hand. Please."

Colin didn't want to let go. He wanted to shake her, but the determination in her face and the way she held her body so rigid told him all he needed to know. She didn't want his help. Nor did she want him holding her back.

Reluctantly, he released her hand and sat up straight. "You know that I care about you."

She shrugged and looked away.

He continued. "We were the Three Musketeers. We did everything together."

Without facing him, she said in a quiet but firm voice, "That was ten years ago. We were kids. Everything is different now."

He didn't want it to be different. Colin realized he'd always loved Emily. That hadn't changed. Now that Alex was gone...

The thought came suddenly. Just as suddenly, he tried to push it back, guilt weighing heavily. He'd loved Alex like a brother. He'd never wished anything but happiness for him and Emily. But he'd been envious and crushed that she'd chosen Alex over him. Ten years had softened the blow, but it hadn't eased the pain. Now that Alex was out of the picture, Colin didn't have the right to move in on the beautiful widow.

But he'd made a promise. Whether she liked it or not, he would help her.

CHAPTER 2

EMILY SAT in the seat beside Colin, twisting the strap of her purse between her fingers. She should have had the sheriff assign a deputy to transport her back to Eagle Rock.

An hour in Colin's proximity could only mean trouble. When he'd wrapped his arms around her and held her, she'd wanted to stay there until all the bad things happening to her went away.

Guilt gnawed at her insides. Alex hadn't been dead for three months, and she was already thinking about Colin and how much she'd missed him over the past ten years. Especially when her marriage had hit rock bottom, and Alex had gotten sullen and secretive.

"What brought you to Bozeman today?" Colin asked, breaking the silence.

Emily started, clutching her purse to her chest.

Then she remembered the packet the attorney had handed her in his office. She pulled it from her purse and stared down at it, a frown pulling her brow low. "I was in Bozeman to meet with the attorney handling Alex's estate. Alex left this packet for me."

"And the attorney is just now getting it to you?"

She nodded. "He was instructed to give it to me three months after Alex's death." Emily glanced across at him. "It was as if Alex knew he was going to die. How did he know that?"

"And you don't know who he was working with?"

She shook her head. "I always asked how his day was, but I never asked who his clients were. But you'd think the sheriff's offices would have found something on his computer. I thought he kept all of his clients' information in his online files."

Colin nodded toward the envelope Emily held in her hand. "Maybe the packet he gave you holds the answer."

"The attorney said I was to open it when I got home." Her fingers toyed with the seal. "Why would he say that?"

"You were driving. Could be he didn't want you to open it until you got home because he didn't want you to get upset and have a wreck," Colin suggested.

Emily stared at the packet, her eyes narrowing. "The people following me didn't attack until I had this envelope in my hands. Before, they'd always followed at a distance."

"Emily, what's in the envelope?"

Unwilling to wait until she reached home, she tore open the large envelope and pulled out the contents. Inside was a single sheet of paper, a key and a small secure digital card. "Just a letter, a key and an SD card."

Her gaze scanned the words on the page.

Dear Emily,

I've always loved you, but from the day we said I do, I felt like I could never have you, heart and soul. Everything I did, I did in an attempt to make you happy. Too late, I realized the only person who could make you happy was you. I'm sorry I got you into this. I pray my connections don't come back to haunt you. Have a beautiful life. You deserve it.

Alex

Tears welled in Emily's eyes and dropped onto the paper she held in her hand. "Oh, Alex, what have you done?"

"Is that from Alex?" Colin asked.

"It is." Emily read the letter aloud. She scrubbed a hand across her eyes. "What do you think he meant by his 'connections'?"

Colin's lips twisted. "I'd say whoever tried to ram you." He shook his head. "Sounds like Alex got mixed up with some bad characters."

Emily looked up at the dark road ahead. "He was an accountant. How does that profession attract unsavory people?" Her fingers curled around the SD card and the key.

"What about the SD card? Maybe it holds the clues you've been searching for. Do you have a computer at home we can plug it into?"

She nodded. "I have my laptop I use for work."

"Good. Hopefully, it'll shed some light on who could be after you."

"But why me? I didn't do anything?"

"Maybe they don't want whatever is on that card to get out."

"How would they know about the card? I just got it."

"You say they didn't attack until you received the package from the attorney."

Emily nodded, then realized he couldn't hear her head rattle in the darkness and answered, "True."

"That has to be it. They don't want whatever is on that card to get out."

She opened her hand and stared at the tiny object in her palm. "You think they rammed my SUV because of what might be on this SD card or what the key might unlock?"

"I'm just guessing at this point. But why else would they go after you now, when Alex has been gone for three months?"

Again, she closed her hand around the card, her lips thinning. "I don't know what's happening. All I know is that I'm tired of being followed, tired of looking over my shoulder, and it's time to nail the people who killed my husband." Her hands clenched into fists. "I'm done being scared."

Colin smiled and murmured, "That's the Emily I remember."

She frowned. "And don't patronize me."

He held up one hand in surrender. "Sorry. It was a compliment. You were always the one taking on the bullies when no one else would stand up to them."

Her lips curled in a smile. "And you bailed me out on more than one occasion."

"Someone had to," he said, his tone wry. "You always picked the biggest, meanest badass to stand toe to toe with."

"Dale Rice wouldn't have hit me," she argued, remembering the day she'd stood up for one of the computer geeks against the school bully.

Rice, a football lineman, could have snapped her in half with one of his meaty fists.

Colin had stepped between them and defused the situation. He had a way of calming the most belligerent foes with his charm or humor.

"What did you tell Dale that day?" Emily asked. "He never bothered me again. In fact, he was actually nice to me and Milton Grimes, the geek he was teasing."

Colin puffed out his chest. "I told him I'd kick his ass if he ever so much as looked cross-eyed at you or Milton."

Emily shot him a disbelieving glance. "No, you did not."

Colin gave a smug smile. "Guess you'll never know."

She glowered at him. "I despise secrets. Secrets came between Alex and me during the last couple years of our marriage. And from what I'm learning, secrets got Alex killed."

"I get it." Colin glanced toward her. "I told Dale that you and Milton were undercover agents for the FBI, and that he was about to blow your cover."

Emily snorted. "Seriously. What did you tell him?"

Colin's eyebrows rose. "Scout's honor. That's what I told him." He made an X with his finger across his chest. "In strict confidence, of course."

Emily stared at Colin for a long moment and shook her head. "I never knew when you were telling the truth or pulling my leg."

"I never pulled your leg when it was important," he said. "I really did tell Dale that you were an FBI agent."

"And he bought it?" Emily chuckled. "He must have taken one too many hits on the football field."

"That would be my guess." Colin slowed as he entered Eagle Rock a few minutes later and turned on the street where Emily and Alex had lived.

When the truck came to a stop in front of the two-story white house with the forest-green shutters, Emily hesitated to get out.

Colin reached into the glove box and extracted a handgun. He dropped down from his seat and rounded the front to her door, pulling it open. "Come on. The sooner we look at what's on that card, the sooner we'll get to the bottom of who might have killed Alex."

She nodded and took the hand Colin extended to her.

A spark of electricity rippled up her arm and through her body, warming her in the cool night air.

Colin had always had that effect on her. When they'd been the Three Musketeers in high school, she'd felt the same energy and had shied away from it, keeping Colin strictly in the friend zone. He made her feel off-balance, awkward in her own skin and unable to control her emotions and physical reactions. Frankly, the way he'd made her feel had scared her.

Emily liked to control her destiny. She didn't like surprises, and she didn't like it when someone made her feel things she didn't understand.

Over the years, she'd come to grips with her control issues and had learned to relax a little when her world spun out of her grasp. For the past two years, she'd lived in constant churn, wondering why Alex had become distant and was keeping secrets.

She'd never learn to relax with Colin holding her hand. Her nerves on edge, she slipped out of her seat, missed her footing on the running board and fell into Colin's arms.

He held her until she could find her feet and stand on her own. Colin stared down into her eyes, the moonlight reflecting off his. "Are you all right?"

No, she was not all right. She'd spent the past ten years focusing on her marriage to Alex. With her husband dead, she shouldn't be feeling anything like she was for Colin. It wasn't right.

Emily pushed away from Colin and smoothed her hair behind her ears. "I'm fine." She dug in her purse for her keys to the house and led the way up the front porch to the door. Her hand shook as she attempted to insert the key into the lock.

Colin took the keyring from her, unlocked the door and pushed it open.

When she started to step inside, he gripped her arm.

"Let me go first," he said.

She nodded. Though she had been entering her house alone for the past three months, she wasn't as eager to do so now. Not after nearly being killed in her own vehicle.

Colin stepped across the threshold. "I'll be right back."

Then, like the trained combative he was, he disappeared into the darkened hallway. A few minutes later, he reappeared and switched on the light. "All clear."

Emily nodded and entered the home she'd shared with her dead husband. "Thanks. I can take it from here now. You don't have to stay." She wanted him to leave. At the same time, she wanted him to stay.

Colin shook his head. "I want to know what's on

that SD card, and I don't feel comfortable leaving you alone. Not after what happened tonight. You could have been killed, or at the least, hurt badly. You can't stay alone."

"I've been alone since Alex's death."

"Have you?" He cocked an eyebrow. "What about the vehicles following you? Is that the kind of company you want hanging around?"

She shivered at the image of her car crushed beneath the weight of the tavern wall. "No."

"Then let me help you. I guarantee Alex would have wanted me to." Colin's voice deepened and he looked away. "He loved you."

Emily snorted. "Did he?"

Colin nodded. "He pulled me aside before your wedding and told me he'd do anything for you. That he loved you so very much. He promised he would never hurt you."

Emily's heart contracted. "Yeah. And where did that get me? He hurt me when he started lying about what he was up to. He hurt me when he refused to trust me with the truth. For the past year, I thought he was having an affair with another woman." Emily threw up her hand. "For all I know, the man who shot him could have done so out of jealous rage. It could have been Alex's lover's husband."

Colin shot a glance her way. "Do you really think he would have cheated on you? The Alex I knew loved you more than life itself."

She snorted. "Then why did he shut me out of his life?"

"How did he do that?" Colin asked, standing in the living room of her home, filling it with his broad shoulders and concerned frown. He'd used that look on her when she'd been mad or sad about something when they were teens.

It always made her want to spill her guts. Now was no different.

"Over a year ago, he quit talking to me. He would leave the house at five in the morning and not return until well after ten at night." Emily shoved a hand through her thick blond hair. "I really thought he was having an affair. I thought if we had a baby, we might save our marriage." She stared at a darkened window. "I accused him of it that night…the night he died. We were arguing, or he might have seen that vehicle coming up beside him sooner. He might have had time to duck…"

"Sweet Jesus, Emily." Colin shook his head. "Had he ducked, that bullet would have hit you. You would be dead."

Her gaze dropped to her feet. "I might as well be." She'd blamed herself for distracting Alex while he'd been driving, second-guessing her role in the crash.

If she hadn't distracted him, he might have performed some evasive maneuvers and escaped the bullet, the crash and his death.

And she might not have lost their baby.

She pressed a hand to her empty belly, the pain of

her loss, still as physical now as it had been when she'd woken in the hospital to the news.

THE PAIN in Emily's face nearly undid Colin. He wanted to pull her into his arms and take away all her sorrow. For a long moment he fought that urge.

He drew in a deep breath. "Where's your laptop?"

Emily glanced around as if in a daze, then grimaced. "I forgot, the state crime lab has it, as well as Alex's computer."

"Okay, then. I have my laptop in my truck. We can use it to look at that card." He started for the door.

When Emily followed, he turned. "Stay inside and don't stand in front of windows."

She frowned. "Why?"

"Someone shot Alex. If they think you have something they don't want to get out..." He swallowed. "Just don't make a silhouette in the window. It makes too easy a target."

Her throat worked as she swallowed hard. "I've never done anything in my life that would make someone want to shoot me. How does this happen?"

Colin shook his head. "I can't say. I hope that SD card will give us a clue." He raised his eyebrows. "Now, are you going to stay out of the line of fire?"

She nodded.

It took exactly thirty seconds for him to retrieve his laptop case from the truck and return to the house.

Emily opened the door, careful to stand aside, out of view of the yard and anyone who might be aiming for her.

Colin resisted the urge to say *good girl*.

Emily closed the door behind him. "You can set your laptop on the kitchen table."

Colin carried it to the table, unwound the charging cable and plugged it into an electrical socket, and then into the computer. He pulled up a chair and booted the laptop. Moments later, the screen blinked to life. He held out his hand.

Emily laid the SD card onto his palm.

A ripple of awareness blasted through him where her fingers touched his skin.

Forcing himself to focus, Colin slipped the SD card into the computer and watched as a couple of files popped up. One was a video file labeled *Watch Me First*.

Colin looked up at Emily. "Ready?"

Emily pulled a chair up beside Colin's and nodded.

He clicked the video file icon and turned up the sound.

Alex appeared on the monitor, looking much older than his thirty-one years. His face appeared haggard, his eyes bloodshot.

Emily let out a soft gasp and pressed her fingers to her lips, tears filling her eyes.

"Hi, Emily. Since you're viewing this video, I can only assume that I'm dead. I didn't want to leave you without telling you how much I love you and how sorry I am for letting you down."

Emily sobbed quietly beside Colin.

He reached for her hand and held it while Alex continued on the computer. He wanted to reach through the screen and wring Alex's neck for making Emily cry.

"I made mistakes. Perhaps the biggest one of all was marrying you. Not because I didn't want it, but because you deserved better. By marrying me, you gave up the chance of finding true love."

"But—"

Alex held up a hand in the video. "Don't lie to yourself. I know you loved me as a friend, and for that I'm grateful. And you did your best to be a good wife to me. You never complained. I tried everything I could to make you love me more than a friend. When you said you wanted a baby, I was willing to do anything to make that happen." He glanced away and then down at his hands.

"And by anything, I mean anything. You didn't know it, but I had a low sperm count. It wasn't your fault we weren't getting pregnant." His mouth curled up in a self-deprecating smirk. "It might have been God's way of telling me I wasn't worthy of having children."

Tears slipped from Emily's eyes.

Every tear hit Colin like a bullet in the chest.

"You were worthy, Alex," Emily said, speaking to

the man on the screen as though he was really there. "You would have been a good father."

"I like to think I'd have made a good father," Alex said. "But since you're watching this now, I assume I never made it to the birth of my child, or I would have redone this video. I never thought we'd get pregnant."

Emily's hand squeezed Colin's, her nails digging into his palm. "Neither did I."

"Those fertility treatments weren't cheap. I knew how much you wanted a child. My accounting business wasn't making enough money to keep trying. With each visit costing us thousands of dollars, I didn't know what else to do. I couldn't tell you I didn't have the money to keep going."

"You should have told me," Emily whispered.

The Alex on the screen shoved a hand through his hair. "In retrospect, I should have told you. Then I wouldn't be in as much trouble as I am. God, I hope that trouble doesn't impact you and the baby."

"Oh, Alex." Emily pressed her knuckles to her lips. "It did."

"Inside the packet the attorney gave you is a key to my safe deposit box at the First National Bank in Bozeman. In that box is the ledger I used to record my transactions with some pretty unsavory people. I skimmed money out of their accounts when they refused to pay me for my work."

Alex winced. "I might have skimmed more than they would have paid me, but I needed the money and they weren't paying on time, which meant I had to take out loans and pay interest in the meantime."

Emily's jaw tightened. "Oh, Alex. You should have told me."

"You won't find any of this information in my company files or my computer. I tracked it all by hand and on paper. If something's happened to me, you can bet one of them was involved. Take the ledger to the police. Let them handle it. And you might want to get out of the state until it all blows over."

"Son of a bitch," Colin murmured, anger surging through him.

Alex shook his head. "Emily, I'm sorry I couldn't be the man who won your heart. I'm sorry for getting into this mess and leaving you and the baby behind. Just know, I loved you with all my heart, and wish you only love and happiness as you move forward in your life." He pressed two fingers to his lips and touched the camera lens. "Take care, sweetheart."

The video clicked off, and the computer screen reverted to the file.

EMILY SAT IN STUNNED SILENCE, her heart hammering so hard in her chest she feared it would pound its way out. The sorrow and regret she'd felt when she'd first seen Alex's face had quickly been replaced by fear and anger.

Alex hadn't trusted her enough to let her know

what had been going on. She would have told him that having a baby wasn't that important. They had each other, that was all that counted.

Instead, he'd made unilateral decisions that had impacted all of them. Alex had paid with his life and that of his unborn child. She closed her eyes and clenched her teeth to keep from screaming out in anger and frustration. She hadn't been given the opportunity to help.

Damn him.

Colin slipped an arm around Emily's shoulders. "Alex is gone," he said. "But you're still alive. You have to keep on living. Alex would have wanted you to." He drew her into his embrace.

Emily laid her cheek against his chest, her fingers curling into his shirt. It felt like it had been forever since she'd been this close to a man. Even when Alex had been alive, he'd been too distant, if not physically...then emotionally.

Colin's thickly muscled chest was solid, reassuring...needed. She curled her fingers into his shirt and breathed in the earthy, musky scent of his aftershave and let herself lean on him.

As a kind of punishment, Emily had shouldered the aftermath of Alex's death on her own, refusing help from anyone, even her sister. She'd blamed herself for what had happened.

Even though she hadn't shot the bullet that had killed him, she hadn't given him the support he'd needed. "I should have forced him to talk to me."

"Alex could be stubborn," Colin said, his breath stirring the tendrils of hair near her ear.

Emily shivered, far too aware of the man holding her than she should be as a widow. Seeing Colin, having his arms wrapped around her, felt so right. She couldn't let herself regret the decision she'd made or worry about the fact Colin's embrace was exactly what she needed at that moment. She'd worry about what that meant later.

CHAPTER 3

COLIN'S BODY reacted immediately to Emily's pressed against it. He tried to squelch his rising desire, but he couldn't. He'd always loved her and had been heartbroken that she'd chosen Alex to spend her life with.

When they'd married, he couldn't be unhappy for the couple. He'd loved Alex like one of his brothers and had wished him and Emily contentment in their union.

Now, as he held Emily in his arms, he couldn't stop himself from taking in every second. No woman had ever measured up to this one. Oh, he'd dated and slept with a few, but none of them had ever touched him like Emily. She'd been his best friend before he'd discovered he was madly in love with her. If he hadn't joined the military, she might have been his, instead of Alex's wife.

He closed his eyes and pushed back that thought. For years, he'd kicked himself for not fighting harder for her. But how could he, when Alex had meant almost as much to him as Emily had?

"Emily..." he started, not really knowing where he would go with his words, but he had to say something.

A phone rang somewhere in another room.

Emily stiffened, her fingernails digging into his chest. On the second ring, she pushed against him. "I'd better get that." On the third ring, she'd moved free of his embrace and left him in the hallway, moving toward the kitchen.

"Hello?" Her voice carried through the house to where he stood, trying to get a grip on his raging libido.

"You already heard about that?" Emily laughed, although the sound was a little strained. "For such a large state, the grapevine is working just fine."

She was quiet while she listened to the voice on the other end of the line.

"Why were you with Sheriff Barron?"

More silence.

"I guess, since they're friends, it makes sense for the two sheriffs to share information," Emily said. "No, I wasn't hurt. Yes, I'm home. No, you don't need to come over." Another pause. "I'm okay. Really. Besides—"

Colin moved toward the sound of Emily's voice and found her pacing in the kitchen with a cordless phone pressed to her ear.

She was walking away from him. When she

turned, her steps faltered. Her gaze met his, the irises darkening. "I'm not alone. I'll be okay."

Colin could hear the sound of someone talking.

"Brenna, really, I'm not being held hostage. If you must know, Colin's here. He drove me home from Bozeman since my car was totaled."

More talking from the phone.

Colin knew Emily's younger sister, Brenna, from when she used to follow them around on their adventures. She was as dark as Emily was light. Her black hair and brown eyes had been so different from Emily's blond and blue. If he hadn't known their parents, he'd have wondered if Brenna had been adopted. Emily took after her fair mother and Brenna after her dark-haired father. Though younger, Brenna had been fiercely protective of her older sister.

When they'd been teens, Colin had found that trait both endearing and irritating. At this moment, he was glad she was concerned about Emily's wellbeing.

"I'll let you know whatever I find out." Emily drew in a deep breath and let it out. "I will. I love you, too." She set the phone in its charger and stared across the room at Colin. "Thank you for giving me a ride home."

He nodded. "It was my pleasure." Before she could continue, he went on. "Now, if you've got an extra blanket, I'll take the couch."

Emily was shaking her head before he finished

talking. "No, Colin. You're not responsible for me. I can—"

"—take care of yourself. Like you did in Bozeman."

"I managed," she said, her voice weak. She lifted her chin and squared her shoulders. "I drove to the most populated place that I could."

"You were lucky to make it to the tavern."

"Yeah, maybe so, but I made it." Her chin tipped a bit higher.

Colin's forehead pinched. "I'm not leaving you alone." He tilted his head toward the door. "If you ask me to leave, I will. But I'll sleep in my truck outside your house. I repeat...I'm not leaving you alone."

Emily's eyes narrowed, and she chewed on her bottom lip for a moment before turning and walking away. "I'll get that blanket. You can stay tonight."

Colin let go of the breath he'd been holding. He'd expected Emily to put up more of a fight. Her near miss must have shaken her more than she was willing to admit aloud.

Hell, it had shaken him more. Had she been a moment or two slower... He turned for the front door. "I'll get my go bag out of my truck."

She glanced over her shoulder. "You brought your go bag?"

He shrugged. "As Marine Force Recon, we had to travel with a go bag of essential items at all times, in case we were called to deploy on a moment's notice."

Her brows knit. "That made it hard to have any kind of life outside the military, didn't it?"

"I suppose." He nodded. "There were a lot of divorces among my teammates."

"I can imagine," Emily said.

"Yeah. There were times I was glad I was the single guy. I didn't have to worry about coming home to find my wife had left me for another guy, taking the children and the dog, while I was out defending the nation." He'd been with several of his buddies through their drinking binges, when they'd tried to drown their anger, disappointment and gut-wrenching sorrow over the loss of their families.

Her eyes rounded. "That happened?"

He gave her a weak smile. "All too often. Some left to go home to their mothers. They couldn't handle being alone or wondering if their husbands would come home on their own two feet, or in a box."

"That's awful," she said, her hands twisting together, her gaze shifting to the windows over-looking the driveway. "You'd think they'd have known what they were getting into and stick it out."

Colin shook his head. "I hated seeing my buddies suffer. The pain of losing a loved one lasted longer than the pain of a wound."

"Having been on the other end of that scenario, I can understand." Emily snorted. "And I thought marrying an accountant was a safe choice," she murmured, the shadows in her eyes darkening. "I'll get that blanket." She spun and walked away.

Colin's gaze followed her up the stairs. When she disappeared into a room on the upper landing, he exited the house and hurried out to his truck, wondering if he was doing the right thing. Being with Emily brought back all the feelings he'd had for her. Having been away for so long had not diminished his longing for the woman at all. In fact, his desire had grown. He wanted to hold her in his arms and keep holding her for a very long time.

Though Colin had wanted Emily in his life, her choice to marry Alex had been the right one for her. Her father, a military man, had died in combat when Emily had been young, leaving behind her mother and sister to make it on their own. She'd always said she never wanted to leave Montana, or the family and friends she had here. They were her roots and the stability she'd always craved.

Colin had known he would enter the military from the time he'd learned to walk. His father had instilled in each of his boys the structure and desire to serve in the military branch of his choice. Each had gone into a different branch, forging his own way, while following their father's footsteps.

Now, they were all back in Montana on leave to find their father.

Colin's gut clenched. His father had been a hard man to live up to, but they all loved him and wanted to see him come home. The longer he remained missing, the slimmer the chances of finding him alive.

Colin stepped out onto the porch and drew in a deep breath of the Montana night air. He'd have to keep a rein on his feelings. Three months wasn't a great deal of time to mourn the death of a husband. And just because Alex was dead didn't make it right for Colin to swoop in and claim Emily as his own. Nothing had changed in the past ten years. Emily still wouldn't want a man who prioritized his career before his family. Even if his career was in defense of his country.

He grabbed the go bag from behind the back seat of his king cab pickup, slung it over his shoulder and headed back to the house, his gaze continuously scanning the immediate vicinity for movement.

No matter what Emily wanted or didn't want, Colin couldn't leave her to defend herself alone. Even if she could take care of herself, she needed someone to have her back when she wasn't looking.

He entered the front door in time to catch Emily descending the staircase with a pillow and a blanket.

She was every bit as beautiful now as she had been when they were in high school. Maybe even more so.

When she handed him the blanket, their hands touched.

A spark of electricity raced up his arm and spread throughout his body.

Her gaze shot to his before her eyelids descended, cloaking her expression and feelings.

Had she felt the spark as well?

His pulse humming through his veins, Colin opened his mouth to ask, but then closed it immediately. He had no right to ask her if she'd felt something more than friendship at their touch. She was the widow of his best friend, and he had to remind himself that was all they could ever be.

"We have a spare bedroom upstairs, if you'd rather sleep in a real bed," she offered.

He'd rather sleep with her.

And there he went, right back to where he had no business going.

"I'll be fine on the couch," he forced out between clenched teeth. "Go to bed." *Before I do something really stupid, like kiss you.*

As soon as that thought popped into his head, heat burned a path from his lips down to his groin.

"Are you sure?" Emily asked.

"Go, Emily," he said, his voice gruff. He nodded toward the staircase. "The sooner you're upstairs, the sooner I can sleep."

"Oh," she said. "Okay, then." She walked toward the front door. "I'll just lock up."

"I'll take care of the doors and check all the windows. Just go." His chest was so tight, he thought it might explode.

She frowned. "Did I say something that made you mad?"

"No," he said tightly, then sighed. He couldn't take out his frustration on the woman who was causing it.

It was his fault he had no control around her. Not hers. "I'm just tired."

Emily gave him one last glance. "Thank you for being there when I needed you. I can't tell you how badly I needed a friend at that exact moment."

"I'm glad I was there as well." But he didn't want to be her friend. Yes, they'd started as friends, but by the time he'd gone to boot camp, he'd known they could never be just friends ever again.

He'd made the mistake of kissing her.

And he wanted to kiss her again. Now. In the house she'd shared with Alex.

His thoughts and desires were all wrong. If he made it through the night without acting on his desires, he'd have to come up with another solution to protecting Emily. He was in Eagle Rock to find his missing father, not to act as Emily's bodyguard. But he wouldn't feel right leaving her safety in the hands of anyone else. He'd made a promise when she'd married Alex that he'd be there for her should anything ever happen to Alex.

Caught between a rock and a hard place, Colin knew what he had to do.

He'd made a promise. He had to protect Emily.

CHAPTER 4

EMILY LAY awake into the night, staring up at the ceiling of the guest bedroom where she'd slept for the past six months, even before Alex's death.

She'd moved into the bedroom right after she'd learned she was pregnant. He'd been coming home from the office later and later at night. She'd hinted at his having an affair, what with his late nights and secretive habits. Alex hadn't shared what he'd been up to, cementing her suspicions that he was indeed having an affair.

When she'd woken up after his death and the death of their unborn baby, she'd wished she could take back all the ugly words they'd thrown at each other. No matter how angry she'd been with him, she hadn't wished him dead.

She didn't know what had happened over the years. They had known each other for so long. When had they stopped being friends?

Images of her, Alex and Colin racing horses across the fields of Iron Horse Ranch came back to haunt her. They'd been so close. All that had changed when they'd become aware of each other as more than best friends.

Colin had kissed her behind the barn one bright sunny day, before Alex had arrived for their afternoon of horseback riding.

Her response to the kiss had scared her so much, she'd made it a point not to be alone with Colin, again. She'd never felt so out of control as she had during that one kiss.

Shortly after she'd kissed Colin, she'd kissed Alex. His kiss had been gentle and nowhere near as explosive as Colin's.

Her father's death, and the resulting instability in her family life, had imprinted a need for her to have control over her fate. Colin's kiss had left her confused and had made her heart pound so hard, she'd thought it would jump out of her chest. She'd decided he was dangerous to her ability to regulate her body, her mind and her future.

When he'd told her he was going into the military, she'd known she couldn't go with him. Her father's death had sent her family into a tailspin. Her mother had never gotten over it. She'd grieved herself into an early grave, passing away from cancer and a broken heart months after Emily graduated high school.

Brenna had been in her sophomore year when their mother had passed. At that same time, Emily hadn't let her heart decide which of her best friends she should marry. Her head led her to choose Alex and stay in Eagle Rock to see Brenna through her last two years of high school. And why not? She'd loved Alex. He'd had always been there for her, just like Colin. Until Colin had left and Alex changed.

Now, Colin lay on the couch downstairs, in the house she and Alex had lived in together.

And her heart beat so fast, Emily thought it would jump from her chest.

She sat up in bed, breathing hard, her lungs unable to keep up with her pulse. What was it about Colin that made her lose focus? Why did she react the way she did around him? Every touch was like a burst of flame, racing through her system.

He frightened her. Not in a horror movie kind of way but in a wild, unfettered way. She should send him away...tell him she would be fine without him. She reached into the nightstand where she kept the loaded .40 caliber pistol Alex had given to her last Christmas.

At the time, Emily had thought it an unusual present. Not anymore.

"Oh, Alex..." she moaned, staring down at the weapon. "What happened? What did you get into?" A sob escaped her. She hadn't realized just how alone she was in this big old house until now. The thought of sending Colin away made it all too real. But he couldn't stay. He owed her nothing. And she couldn't rule her own thoughts and feelings whenever he was near.

The crack of floorboard sounded outside her door.

Emily's breath caught in her throat, and her heartbeat quickened. In the dim moonlight streaming through the window, she could see the doorknob turn.

Her hand shaking, Emily raised the gun, aiming it at the door. She thumbed the safety lever and waited for the door to open.

Had the person who'd been following her found her in her own home? If so, how had he gotten past Colin?

Dear God. Had he hurt Colin?

Emily's hand steadied, and her thundering pulse slowed. She sat up straighter and stared across the shadowy room as the door slowly swung open.

With her finger resting lightly on the trigger, she focused all her attention on the intruder.

"Emily?" a voice whispered. Colin appeared in the doorway, barefooted, wearing only his half-buttoned jeans.

"Are you out of your mind?" she cried, pulling her finger out of the trigger and switching the safety on. "I almost shot you."

He chuckled, leaning against the doorjamb. "That wouldn't have been the first time I've been shot."

Emily dragged in a deep breath and willed her suddenly racing heartbeat to return to normal.

However, seeing Colin bare-chested and standing so near to her bed only made her pulse race faster.

His dark brow dipped, and he entered the room, stopping beside her bed. "Emily, are you okay?"

Hell no, she wasn't. Not when he was standing so close, all those naked muscles bathed in the blue light from the moon.

"I'm fine," she said, her breathing coming in short rapid breaths. "I thought you might be an intruder."

"I wouldn't let anyone pass me to get to you," he assured her, brushing a strand of her hair back from her cheek.

"I thought you might have been injured. I was ready to pull the trigger and kill the bastard."

His low chuckle warmed her inside, sending heat all the way to her core. "You were worried about me?"

She shrugged and moved the pistol from her lap to the nightstand. "You're not invincible, you know," she said, her voice low and annoyed. "No one is."

Colin touched her shoulder. "Scoot over."

"Why?"

"Because my feet are cold, and I want to sit." His brow twisted. "Unless I'm making you uncomfortable. Is that it? Do I make you uncomfortable, Emily?"

Yes, he did. But she wasn't about to admit it. "No. Of course not." She inched over on her bottom, giving Colin enough room on the edge of the bed.

He lowered himself until he sat beside her,

tucking his feet beneath the sheets. Then he slipped his arm around her shoulders. "There. Isn't that better?"

"For who?" she grumbled, loving the feel of his body close to hers, the vague scent of his aftershave teasing her senses.

"For me, of course. I shouldn't admit it, but I sleep better in my boots. At least then, my feet don't get as cold."

Typical Colin. He made her laugh when she was at her most disturbed. "That's such an old man thing to say. Have you considered sleeping in a pair of socks? My mother did that."

"And ruin my reputation as a ladies' man?" He shook his head. "No way." His arm tightened around her shoulders. But not so much that she couldn't get away, if she really wanted.

And she didn't want to.

"But seriously," he said. "I didn't come back to Iron Horse Ranch to die."

Her eyes welled with tears. "I've had four of the people I love die. I'm beginning to think it's me. I'm the common factor in all of their lives and deaths." Her eyes widened. "Brenna. Oh, sweet Jesus. What if—"

Colin tipped up her chin. "Sweetheart, not everyone around you is going to die. And those who have, didn't die because of you."

She gave a very unladylike snort. "How could it not be me?" A sob rose up her throat. She tried hard to swallow it back down but failed miserably. Tears welled in her eyes and slipped unchecked down her cheeks. "What's wrong with me?"

"Nothing is wrong with you. Your father gave his life for his country and the safety and freedom of his children. Your mother died of a terrible disease. As for Alex, we need to figure out what happened there." He kissed her forehead. "The main thing you need to remember is that none of these things were your fault."

She shook her head, knowing he was right, yet her losses made it hard to believe she wasn't the cause. "I couldn't live if you or Brenna are harmed."

"We're okay. And we're going to stay okay." He brushed his lips across the tip of her nose. "Right now, you need to sleep. In the morning, we'll start searching for answers."

She sniffed. For the first time in a while, she felt a spark of hope. "But you're here to find your father."

"We'll kill two birds with one stone. While I'm asking around about my father, we'll ask questions about Alex." He stared down into her eyes.

Emily fell into his gaze, wishing life had turned out differently than it had.

"I'm going to help you find Alex's killers," Colin said.

"And I'll help you find your father," Emily replied, her voice fading into a whisper as Colin's lips descended to sweep a feathery kiss across her mouth.

"Now, sleep," Colin said, his voice gruff. "Before I forget you were the wife of my best friend."

"We were all best friends before I married Alex," she reminded him.

He gave a curt nod, settled his head back against the headboard and closed his eyes. "I'm trying to remind myself of that, every minute I'm near you. Please, quit talking. You're making it hard for me to focus on sleep."

Emily lay still in his arms, reveling in the warmth of his skin against hers. Sleep didn't come quickly. She lay listening to Colin's breathing, wishing he would kiss her again.

It wasn't until Colin was fully asleep that Emily could relax. Then sometime during the early morning hours, her sleep filled with nightmares about the day Alex died.

She woke in Colin's arms, her cheek pressed to his naked chest, his arm flung across her midsection.

For a long moment, she considered moving away, giving him space. The lingering horror of seeing her husband's blood on her clothes, and waking to the news she'd lost her baby, kept her close. She needed the strong arm around her and the solid body beneath her cheek. Colin grounded her at the same time as he sent her spiraling out of control.

Emily didn't care. She was glad she'd found him in that bar in Bozeman when she had. Fate must have drawn her to him.

Again, Emily slept.

. . .

THE SOUND of glass shattering woke Colin just before dawn. His arm had fallen asleep beneath Emily's head and tingled sharply.

He extricated his arm from beneath Emily, waking her in the process.

"What's wrong?" she whispered.

"I heard something that sounded like breaking glass." He swung his legs over the side of the bed and stood on the cool hardwood floor, wishing he'd slept in his boots.

Emily rolled out of bed on the other side, pulling her robe over her shoulders, and slipped her feet into a pair of hard-bottomed slippers. "You can't go downstairs barefooted." She crossed to where he stood.

"I can't stay up here," he said and crossed to the open door.

"At least, take this." Emily placed her .40 caliber pistol in his large hand.

He curled his fingers around it. "Thanks."

Leaning across the threshold, he paused and listened. Nothing stirred below, but the acrid scent of gasoline tickled his senses, and smoke rose from the first floor.

"I'd say stay here," Colin said. "But I think your house is on fire. Follow me, but not too closely, in case we have an intruder."

Her eyes widened in the darkness, but she nodded and waited for him to step out.

Colin led the way down the stairs, hurrying toward the living room and the smoke filling the air.

In the hallway, he hurriedly shoved his feet into his cowboy boots and continued to the living room. Broken glass littered the wood flooring where the remnants of a bottle lay shattered against a wall and flames consumed the gasoline the bottle had contained.

A light, lace curtain billowed in the breeze rushing through a broken window, fanning the flames now crawling up the side of an upholstered armchair.

"Oh, sweet Jesus," Emily cried and started forward.

Colin held up a hand. "Don't come any closer. You'll silhouette yourself against the window." He grabbed a quilted blanket from the back of a lounge chair and threw it over the flames. Then he stomped on it until the fire was out.

"Colin!" Emily cried out. "Look out! He's got a gun!"

Colin ducked low a moment before a shot was fired through the shattered window.

He hunkered low and ran for the entrance. "Stay out of sight," he called out as he ripped open the front door and ran out into the night.

As soon as he was outside, he leaped off the porch

and ran in the direction of the living room window through which the shooter had fired.

He couldn't see anyone in the immediate vicinity and rounded the side of the house in time to see a man leaping onto a motorcycle. Another motorcycle shot out of the yard and out onto the street.

Colin powered up, running as fast as he ever had, determined to catch the man still trying to start his bike.

On his second attempt to start the engine, it engaged. The bike rider twisted the throttle at the exact moment Colin caught up with him.

Colin leaped onto the man's back, grabbed his shoulders and dragged him backward.

The man held onto the handlebar. The motorcycle popped a wheelie and raced away without its rider.

Colin and the intruder hit the ground hard.

Immediately, the shooter rolled and threw a punch. His fist grazed Colin's cheek.

Colin punched him in the nose and cocked his arm to swing again. The man kicked him in the gut, sending him flying backward.

Then the assailant broke free, rolled to his feet and ran for the motorcycle that had crashed to the ground twenty yards away.

Adrenaline dulled the pain in his belly long enough for Colin to run after the man.

The man lifted the bike and slung his leg over the seat when Colin caught him

This time, when Colin tried to pull him off the bike, he held tight. Colin refused to let him get away and hung on, his feet dragging across the grass.

In the struggle, the motorcycle veered toward a tree. The driver yelled, "Let go!"

Colin refused, praying the man would stop the bike before they hit the tree.

At the last moment, Colin let go, dropped to the ground and rolled, coming up on his feet.

The driver jerked the steering wheel to the right. Too late. The bike slammed into the tree. The rider flew over the handlebars and crashed, head-first, into the trunk with a sickening crunch.

Colin ran to the unconscious man and bent to feel for a pulse. After a long moment he felt the soft bump of blood pumping through the attacker's carotid artery.

"Colin!" Emily called out from the front porch.

"Call 911," he yelled. "And get back inside."

"Calling," she replied and disappeared back into the house, closing the door behind her.

Not long afterward, the wail of sirens preceded the arrival of a sheriff's vehicle, followed by an ambulance.

Colin stood, waving the vehicles over to where the man lay on the ground, unmoving.

Sheriff Barron emerged from his service vehicle and approached Colin.

"What's happened?"

Emily came out of the house and joined the sheriff, her hands clutched together, her eyes wide as she stared at Colin. "Oh, thank God, you're all right."

"More than I can say for this guy." Colin moved to the side, pointing at the man who'd tried to escape but had lost the fight with a tree.

"I thought I saw two motorcycles," Emily said, glancing around.

"The other one got away," Colin said.

"Start at the beginning, while the EMTs do their thing." The sheriff took out a pad of paper and a pen.

Colin filled him in on the Molotov cocktail, the shots fired and the subsequent chase and escape.

Sheriff Barron shook his head. "Think this has anything to do with the attack in Bozeman?"

"That would be my guess." Colin's gaze met Emily's.

She nodded. "I think it also has something to do with Alex's death."

The sheriff tilted his head to one side. "Got any proof?"

"Well...no," Emily said. "But—"

"Can't arrest anyone on gut instinct," he said. "I need solid facts to make any headway."

Emily's lips pressed together in a thin line. "I don't have any facts. But before Alex died, the only things trying to kill me were the bloodsucking mosquitoes. Since Alex's death, I've had someone following me everywhere I've gone. Tonight, after a visit to our attorney, suddenly, I have others willing to risk their lives in an effort to kill me. What have I done to garner such hatred?"

"It might not be hatred at all," the sheriff said. "What transpired at the attorney's office?"

Emily shot a look at Colin. "He gave me a packet with a letter, and SD card and a key." She told him about the video on the SD card.

Sheriff Barron rubbed his chin. "If Alex was playing with the wrong kids on the playground, they might have concluded that he'd shared his toys with you. These guys might think you know something. Or they're being paid by someone who thinks you know something. Something they don't want to get out."

"You think someone might have paid those two to torch Emily's house?" Colin asked.

The sheriff shrugged. "Seemed pretty amateur to me." He tipped his head toward Emily. "I'd like to see that video and know what you find in that safe deposit box."

"I'll let you know as soon as I find out myself." Emily raised her chin. "I plan on being in Bozeman when that bank opens this morning."

"Need an escort?" the sheriff asked.

Colin cupped Emily's arm. "I'm going with her."

The sheriff's eyes narrowed. "Armed?"

"Damn right," Colin responded. After all that had happened, he'd be a fool to go without some kind of weapon.

"Good," the sheriff said. "Miss Emily needs

looking after until we figure out who's sending their lackies to do their bidding. Any luck on finding the girl with the unicorn tattoo?"

Colin nodded. "I have a couple leads. While we're in Bozeman, I'll follow up on them."

"I know a state police detective is working the case," the sheriff said, "but from what I've heard, their caseloads are insane. It doesn't hurt to have more people sifting through any evidence we can find." He stared from Emily to Colin and back. "Again, if you hear anything, let me know."

Emily nodded.

Colin held out his hand. "We will."

The sheriff clasped it and held on longer than necessary. "It goes both ways. If I hear anything about your father or Miss Emily's attacker, I'll let you know."

Sheriff Barron gave her crooked smile. "I remember the day your mama brought you back to Eagle Rock. I never wanted her to regret that day one bit."

The sheriff and his deputies gathered the bottle fragments from the Molotov cocktail and had the motorcycle hauled off to the impound lot to be investigated. If their guy didn't wake up from the crash, then hopefully, they'd learn who owned the bike and follow any leads to who sent him to burn Emily's house...with her in it.

From what Colin could tell, the bike didn't have a license plate. And he'd bet his paycheck the serial number had been scratched off. Their best hope was the guy recovering enough to answer some questions.

"I'll be in Bozeman at the hospital to wait for this guy to come to." The sheriff handed Colin a business card. "Here's my personal cell phone number. Call me. I'll let you know what I find out about our motorcycle rider."

Colin shared a hard look with the sheriff then gave him a curt nod.

"Thank you, sheriff," Emily said.

The sheriff's men wrapped up their investigation, and the emergency responders left with the motorcycle rider, headed for Bozeman.

Colin led Emily back into the house. "Got a hammer, scrap lumber and nails?"

She shrugged. "Alex kept all his tools in the garage. I think he had some wood left over from work he did on the deck." She closed her eyes and pushed a hand through her blond hair. The dark circles beneath her eyes were even darker than they'd been before she'd gone to bed the evening before.

"I'll do something about the window. Why don't you go to bed and get whatever sleep you can before our trip to Bozeman?"

She shook her head, her gaze going to the blanket on the floor of her living room. The stench of gasoline and smoke permeated the air. "I couldn't sleep, even if I wanted. I'll work on cleaning up this mess while you work on the broken window."

"At least, let me help you pick up the glass, before I fix the window."

"Suit yourself. I just can't leave it there." She entered the kitchen and secured a broom and a dustpan.

Colin grabbed the kitchen trash can and followed Emily back to the living room.

Together, they gathered all the broken glass the sheriff's department had considered too small to collect and placed it into the trash container.

"What do you want me to do with the blanket?" Colin lifted the quilt off the floor. Some of the patches had been blackened by the fire. Others were burned all the way through.

Emily shook her head and pointed to the trash. "You might as well throw it away. It's ruined." Her eyes filled with tears. "My grandmother made that for me as a wedding present. She died the next year from complications from pneumonia."

Colin froze the hand holding the blanket over the trashcan. "I'm not throwing away something your grandmother made for you."

"I wouldn't know how to fix it. I never learned how to sew." Her lips quirked upward at the corners. "I was too busy riding horses with two of the county's worst hooligans to learn."

Colin grinned. "I'll ask my mother if she knows a quilter who could fix it." He folded the blanket and carried it into the kitchen. In the pantry, he found a plastic trash bag, stuffed the quilt inside and carried it out to his truck.

When he returned to the house, he found the tools he needed in the garage, cut a sheet of plywood to fit the broken window and screwed it into the frame. At least that one window couldn't be used again to toss a Molotov cocktail into.

There were still twenty or more windows an arsonist could target. Glass was easily broken.

While he'd worked on covering the window, Emily scrubbed and mopped the floor and walls, removing as much of the soot as she could with a strong cleaning fluid. The scent of smoke warred with a lemony floor cleaner.

By the time they had done what they could, the gray light of dawn edged out the darkness and started to fill the sky over the tops of the mountain ridges surrounding the town.

"Are you hungry?" Emily asked.

Colin's stomach rumbled loudly. "Yeah. Let's get cleaned up, and I'll treat you to breakfast at the diner. Then we can head into Bozeman in time for the bank to open."

"You're on. There are two showers, so you don't have to wait on me." She gave him a weary smile. "Thanks for being here."

He reached out and gripped her arms. The thought of her being alone when that Molotov cocktail had hit the window made his stomach clench. Had she not found him in that bar in Bozeman, he might not have been here for her. She could have died in the fire.

Colin pulled her into his arms and held her tight. "I'm glad I was here." He held her for another minute. Reluctantly, he set her at arms' length. "I bet I shower faster than you."

She chuckled. "Is that a challenge? You know I always beat you."

He winked. "I always let you."

She leaned up on her toes and pressed her lips to his in a brief kiss. "Game on." Emily spun and raced up the stairs.

Colin stood for a long time, staring at the empty staircase, knowing he was getting in over his head. But he couldn't back out now. He had to see this through until she was safe again.

In the meantime, he feared his soul would take a beating, and he wasn't sure he'd live through the heartache a second time.

CHAPTER 5

EMILY DIDN'T STOP RUNNING until she'd reached the bathroom in the master suite and closed the door behind her. She leaned against the back of the door, needing its support to keep her shaking knees from buckling.

What had she been thinking? Why had she kissed Colin? She knew better.

As with the first time they'd kissed, her heart hammered, her gut knotted, and she broke out in a sweat.

She'd never felt this discombobulated when she'd kissed Alex. Once again, she was scared.

And exhilarated.

And more alive than she'd felt in months. Maybe years.

She pressed her knuckles to her lips where they still tingled from touching Colin's.

Yeah, she'd felt something when she'd touched him, when their lips had met. But had he? Could what she felt be completely one-sided?

God, it's wrong, wrong, wrong.

Her husband hadn't been dead long. She shouldn't be experiencing such strong emotions about another man.

She pushed away from the door and faced herself in the mirror. What wife could go from one man to another so soon?

She stared into her own eyes and answered the unspoken question.

The worst wife imaginable.

She'd known the truth for ten years, but had never admitted it to anyone, including herself.

It had always been Colin. She'd loved him as long as she'd known him. And not as a brother. That one kiss, so long ago, had brought the truth home. But she'd been so scared by her father's death and her mother's heartbreak, she'd refused to let herself love anyone as much as her mother had loved her father.

That was the real reason why she'd been so afraid. She'd loved Colin so much it physically hurt.

That she still might didn't change anything. She was a recent widow. He'd been gone for ten years. He probably didn't feel the same way. Even if he did, he wouldn't move in on his best friend's widow. He was an honorable man.

Emily turned on the water in the shower and

stripped out of her smoky pajamas and robe. She stepped beneath the cool spray, purposely keeping the heat down to bring her own body temperature under control.

She couldn't let herself go down a path that would lead to heartache. Colin was home to find his father. When John McKinnon was found, Colin would return to his world in the Marine Corps and Emily would remain in Eagle Rock.

For what?

For her sister, for one. Brenna needed her. Emily was her only family.

Never mind that Brenna had a job in real estate and was doing well for herself. She had her little house in Eagle Rock, and she was making it on her own.

"Face it, Em," she said to herself. "Brenna doesn't need you anymore. You've completed your big sister duties." It was time to move on and let Brenna live her life without having a sister to hover over.

But how soon was too soon to get back in the dating market? Three months, six months or a year?

Did it matter how much time had passed since his death? She and Alex's relationship had been strained for the past couple of years.

Emily switched off the shower, toweled dry and looked around the bathroom, her mouth twisting into a wry grin.

She'd been in such a hurry to get out of the same

airspace as Colin, she'd forgotten to get her clothes for the day. Her dirty clothes were in a small pile on the floor, too soiled to wear without first washing.

And her clothes were in the guest bedroom, across the hall from the other bathroom.

Wrapping the towel around her middle and tucking the corner in at her breast, she cracked open the master bedroom door and peered down the hallway.

The coast was clear. If she hurried, she could make it to the bedroom she'd been sleeping in. The one she'd moved her clothing into.

With cool air hitting her naked legs and blowing up her thighs to her equally bare bottom, she scooted down the hallway. The thought of getting caught was both frightening and exhilarating.

As she reached for the doorknob to her bedroom door, Colin hurried out of the bathroom and bumped into her, knocking her off balance.

To keep from slamming into the wall, Emily released her hold on the towel and braced her hands on the wall, catching her fall.

Fortunately, she saved herself from injury. Unfortunately, she suffered the humiliation of her towel coming completely undone and sliding from her body.

She snatched at the fabric and missed.

Colin stood so close, she couldn't bend to retriever her towel without bumping into him. She stood completely naked in front of the man she had just admitted to herself that she'd always loved.

A smile curled the corners of his lips as his gaze slipped over her breasts, down to that tuft of hair covering her sex and quickly back up to her eyes.

Rather than cover herself with her hands, Emily lifted her chin. "If you could hand me my towel…?"

His smile broadened. He bent, snagged the towel and rose, ever so slowly, his face within inches of her thighs, her hips, her ribs and breasts.

When she reached for the towel, he jerked it away.

"Why should I give this to you?" he said, his eyebrows raised.

She swallowed hard. "Because you're a gentleman, and a gentleman always protects the lady."

He looked from side to side. "I don't see that you're in any danger."

Her chin rose. "Maybe not now. Not from others. But I sense danger…" she lowered her voice and admitted, "when I'm with you." Heat rose up her neck and spread throughout her face. At the same time, warmth built at her core.

Holding the towel away from her, he touched her cheek with the backs of his knuckles. "Oh, baby, I know exactly where you're coming from."

She raised an eyebrow. "You do?"

"Mmm." The hand he'd been smoothing along the side of her cheek turned and cupped her chin. "Danger is the operative word here. I'm definitely feeling it now." He bent to touch his lips to her forehead. He let them linger for a moment. Then he sighed, wrapped the towel around her and stepped back.

Emily swayed toward him as if gravity pulled her in. The cool air between them slowly brought her back to her senses.

Clutching the towel around her, she turned and entered the room. As she closed the door, she shot a glance back out into the hallway.

Colin still stood where he'd been, his gaze on her, his eyes inscrutable.

Once the door was closed between them, Emily drew in a shaky breath. Her entire body was on fire. Never in the ten years she'd been married to Alex had she felt this kind of heat. This desire.

She wasn't sure how she could face him again after he'd seen her naked. That thought didn't slow her from dressing quickly and pulling on her shoes.

As embarrassed as she'd been to be caught naked in the hallway, she was still anxious to see Colin again. Was she just a glutton for punishment?

Wearing jeans, a soft baby-blue sweater and a pair of riding boots, she combed the tangles out of her hair and blew it dry. After applying mascara and a dab of lipstick on her mouth, she felt ready to face the man who turned her inside out.

Her hand paused on the doorknob, her pulse racing. Would he be standing outside her door? How easy would it be to drag him into the bedroom and make sweet love to him?

Sweet Jesus, what was wrong with her? Colin was an honorable man. He wouldn't make a move on his friend's widow.

Emily cursed beneath her breath and yanked open the door.

Thankfully, Colin wasn't standing there, giving her a few extra moments to pull herself together before seeing him again.

The scent of bacon drifted up from the first floor.

Emily's stomach rumbled. Alex had never cooked breakfast for her. She usually cooked for him, getting up earlier and earlier to make that happen. When she'd moved out of their bedroom, she'd stopped getting up that early.

Alex hadn't complained. He'd left before she'd gotten up and hadn't gotten home until late at night, long after a reasonable dinnertime.

Following the smell of breakfast cooking, Emily descended the stairs, cringing at the lingering odor of soot and gasoline. It would take a lot more cleaning to eradicate that scent.

The frying bacon helped to mask it, if only for a little while.

As she entered the kitchen, Emily's breath caught in her throat.

Colin stood with his back to her, one hand holding the handle of the skillet, the other wielding a spatula as he fished crispy bacon out of the grease.

"I thought, since you had the ingredients, we'd just eat here and get on the road sooner." He set the bacon on a plate covered with a paper towel. "If you could butter the toast and fill the glasses with orange juice, I'll have the eggs cooked in no time.

The bread popped up from the toaster on cue.

"I can do that." Emily pulled the butter from the refrigerator and a knife from a drawer close to where Colin stood. Her shoulder brushed his, causing a lightning bolt to shoot through her nervous system. She dropped the knife, narrowly missing her foot.

"You okay?" he asked, glancing over his shoulder, a frown creasing his brow.

"I'm fine," she answered quickly.

Emily scooped up the knife, tossed it into the sink and got out another. This time she made it all the way to the toaster without losing it.

She had to get a grip. There were lots more important things to worry about. Drooling over her old friend wasn't one of them.

By the time she buttered the bread and poured orange juice into two glasses, he had the eggs fried to a perfect over-easy, sliding them onto clean white plates.

Emily carried the orange juice to the little kitchen table in the corner and returned to the counter for the toast.

She and Colin settled onto the bright red vinyl seats at the vintage Formica-topped table she'd found in an estate sale several years ago.

"I like the table," Colin said. "It reminds me of the one my grandmother had in her house."

Emily plucked a piece of toast from the stack and laid it on the plate beside her eggs. "I remembered that time she invited the three of us to have lunch with her. I loved that table so much that when I saw this one, I knew I had to have it."

Colin tilted his head to one side. "I wonder what happened to that old table." He stared at the one beneath his plate.

"I found this one in an estate sale at Old Mrs. Belamy's home when she passed."

"My grandmother's table had a nick in the surface from where my father had banged his fork into it once too often as a toddler." He ran his fingers over the surface.

"I remember her telling us that story," Emily said softly, memories of a simpler time filling her with warmth.

"This one is in better shape." Colin glanced up. "It suits you."

"Alex didn't think so. He thought it was too old-fashioned." She smiled weakly. "He wanted me to donate it to the Bozeman Women's shelter." Emily smoothed her hand across the surface. "I dragged my feet." She'd planned on taking it, but Alex had been shot. He was gone, and the table stayed.

She forced herself to eat some of the eggs Colin had cooked, all the while memories of better times warred with memories of her marriage. It hadn't all been bad. Alex really had loved her and had tried to make her happy.

A hand slid across the table and covered hers.

She hadn't realized she'd set her fork down until Colin's fingers curled around hers.

"I'm sorry about what happened to Alex," he said softly.

"Me, too," she replied. "And I'm sorry about everything that led up to it. If he hadn't been trying so hard to make me happy, he wouldn't have gotten into this mess. He wouldn't be dead."

Emily looked up, meeting Colin's gaze.

"This isn't your fault," Colin assured her. "Alex made poor choices. Someone else pulled the trigger. You didn't."

"I might as well have." Emily tugged her hand from beneath his, gathered her plate full of uneaten eggs and carried it to the counter. "I'll do the dishes when I get back from Bozeman. We should get moving."

Colin rose from the table and carried his plate over, setting it beside Emily's. Once his hands were free, he gripped her arms. "You have to believe it. You didn't cause any of this to happen."

She shook her head. "Not directly. But I did indirectly. If I had loved Alex as much as he loved me, none of this would've happened. He'd be alive. We'd have been a happily married couple, growing old together."

Colin tipped up her chin. "Lots of people marry

too young and discover too late they aren't suited as a couple. You two were young."

"Yeah, but I should've known better than to marry my best friend. Not only did I make his life miserable, I lost my best friend."

"I thought I was your best friend, too."

Emily drew in a deep breath. "You were…"

"Were?" His brow furrowed.

She nodded. "Until you kissed me."

He stood for a long time, holding her arms in his grasp. "I'd say I was sorry…" he shook his head, "but I can't. I've never been surer of kissing someone in my entire young life. I am sorry, however, if it made you uncomfortable."

She stared up into his eyes, afraid he'd see the truth. More afraid that he'd miss it. "It made me very uncomfortable."

"You should have told me."

"You were on your way out of Eagle Rock. I was scared." She shrugged. "Alex was safe."

"I'm not sorry I kissed you. I could never be sorry about that." He let go of her arms and stepped backward. "I would never have kissed you, had I known it would have frightened you so much."

She snorted. "You must have missed the fact that I kissed you back. It doesn't matter now." With a wave of her hand, she pushed the past to where it belonged. "But we have bigger fish to fry than teenaged kissing. You need to find your father, and I need to see what's in that safe deposit box."

And talking about kissing wasn't making it any easier to keep from repeating the mistake.

Newly widowed women shouldn't go around kissing men. Especially, when the man was the one who'd kept her from fully loving her deceased husband. Not that she'd ever tell him that. What good would it serve?

CHAPTER 6

AFTER CAREFULLY CHECKING the surroundings and deeming it safe for Emily to come out of her house, Colin led the way to his truck.

Once he had Emily safely positioned in the passenger seat, he climbed into the driver's seat and drove out of Eagle Rock, headed for Bozeman.

They accomplished the long drive in relative silence.

As they neared Bozeman, Colin glanced at the clock on the dash. "The bank won't be open for another forty-five minutes. Want to see if the sheriff has had a chance to interview your arsonist?"

"Good idea."

He headed for the hospital, passing the bank as he did.

Emily's gaze locked in on the bank as they passed. "I wonder if the people who attacked my house last night know there's a ledger in the bank."

"If they do, you won't be safe going in." Colin frowned. He didn't like the fact Emily was a target. "We'll have to think that through."

They arrived at the hospital with forty minutes to spare until the bank opened.

As Colin climbed down from his seat, he spied Sheriff Barron's service vehicle near the entrance. "Looks like the sheriff is here."

"Great. Maybe he can shed more light on who's behind the attacks." Emily started to slide out of her seat.

"Hold on. Let me get around to you before you get out."

"I'm capable of climbing out of a truck on my own."

He chuckled as he closed his door and hurried around to her side of the truck. "I know you're capable, but you're not bullet-proof."

She frowned as he handed her down from her seat. "What? So, you think you're going to be my shield?" Emily shook her head. "I don't want you taking a bullet for me."

"You said it," he reminded her. "It's what a gentleman would do." Then he winked. "My protecting you is a deterrent."

"If they want me dead, they'll take you out to get to me." She touched a finger to his chest. "I refuse to be responsible for another man's death."

He captured her finger in his and pressed a kiss to the tip. "Again, you aren't responsible for anyone's death. And most certainly not my potential demise. You aren't pulling the trigger."

"Shut up and step away from me. If someone is determined to shoot me, I don't want you caught in the crossfire." She stepped out, trying to get ahead of him.

Colin easily caught up to her and cupped her elbow in his palm. "You're still as stubborn as you were at seventeen."

"I'll take that as a compliment," she said, her chin held high.

They entered the hospital and crossed to the information desk where they found the sheriff talking to the volunteer behind the counter.

She was just giving him the room number.

When the sheriff turned toward the elevator, he spied Colin and Emily. "Ah, good. I'm glad to see you two. I just got word that our arsonist-shooter regained consciousness. I was on my way up to question him."

"Mind if we come along?" Colin asked.

"Not at all," the sheriff said. "Though you'll have to wait outside his room while I conduct my interview."

"Fair enough," Emily said. "Though I'd like to hear his answers. After all, it was my house he tried to burn down and my life he tried to end."

Colin chuckled. Trust Emily to throw sarcasm into the mix.

As the elevator door slid open, the sheriff gave

her a crooked smile. "Understood. But you're not law enforcement. This is my job."

Emily stepped into the elevator car. "I understand. We'll wait outside the room."

Colin followed her in.

The sheriff was the last to climb in, hitting the button for the floor where his prisoner was located. "I'll let you know whatever I find out. Did you have any more trouble after we left last night?"

"No, sir," Colin responded. Only a sleepless night filled with a tremendous desire to pull Emily close and hold her until the danger went away.

The elevator stopped on their floor.

As the door slid open, a scream sounded in the hallway.

The sheriff pulled his service revolver and ran out into the hall.

A woman wearing blue scrubs raced toward the nurse's station. "Code blue. Code blue! Someone got past the guard. The prisoner isn't breathing."

Sheriff Barron ran for the room number he'd been given.

A man dressed in a county sheriff's uniform struggled to rise to his feet from the floor with the help of a nurse. He had an ugly gash on his forehead and blood dripping down his face. "I'm sorry, sir," he said as the sheriff approached. He pointed to a tall food tray cart. "He pushed the food cart by, and before I knew it, he hit me in the head with something hard." The deputy pressed his fingers to the wound and winced.

"Let us take care of that," the nurse said.

"In a minute," the deputy said and pushed past her and into the room. "I must have blacked out. What happened to the—"

Inside the room, several people were bent over the man in the bed. One had paddles in her hands. "Clear!" she called out and applied the paddles to the man's chest.

The man's body lurched as a charge of electricity jolted him.

The nurses standing by stared at the heart monitor. A green line crept straight across.

"Again," the nurse holding the paddles called out. "Clear!"

Everyone stood back as she applied the paddles again. And, again, the man's body rocked in the bed.

The green line remained flat.

A doctor arrived, pushing through the crowd gathered at the door.

An older nurse moved toward the people gathered in the doorway. "Everyone out. Please. Wait in the lounge. We'll keep you informed."

The sheriff, deputy, Colin and Emily backed away from the door, leaving the medical staff to do their work.

"I'm sorry, sir," the deputy said. "I didn't see it coming. He was dressed in scrubs like everyone else. I thought he was delivering food to patients."

"You couldn't have known," the sheriff said.

"What did he look like?" Colin asked. "Besides the scrubs?"

The deputy shook his head slowly. "He had dark hair and a goatee. And I think I saw a tattoo on his right forearm." He shook his head. "I wish I'd paid more attention." He swayed.

The sheriff grabbed his arm to steady him. Then he snagged a nurse as she passed him in the hallway. "Can we get someone to take care of this man?"

She stared up at the deputy's forehead. "He should go to the emergency room. That big a cut might need stitches, and we're not equipped to perform sutures in this department."

The sheriff nodded and turned to the deputy. "You heard the lady. You're going down to the ER."

"I'll get a wheelchair," the nurse offered.

"I can walk," the deputy argued.

"Look," the nurse planted a fist on her hip, "I'll get you down the ER in a wheelchair, or not at all. I don't have time to argue or pick your sorry ass off the hospital floor."

The deputy grinned and winced. "Okay, okay, you don't have to be so cranky."

"Want me to go with you?" the sheriff asked.

The deputy shook his head, cringing. "No. I can take care of this. You need to be here to learn our prisoner's fate."

The sheriff gently clapped the man on his shoulder. "We'll get to the bottom of this."

Colin glanced down at Emily. "Stay with the sheriff. I need to check on something."

She frowned. "What do you need to check on?"

"I left my phone in my truck," he lied.

Her frown deepened. "I'll go with you."

"No," he said. "I'll be right back. No use going all the way down to the parking lot. Besides, you'll want to know what happened to the prisoner as soon as they come out of there."

Emily chewed on her bottom lip. "Okay. But don't be gone long. We have to make it to the bank when it opens."

Colin didn't respond. He left Emily standing in the hallway with the sheriff. Instead of taking the elevator, he took the stairs to the ground floor, careful not to touch the bars across the doors if he could help it.

If the guy who hit the deputy and then attacked the prisoner wanted to get out of the hospital, he'd have taken the stairs instead of the elevator. He'd get to the ground floor faster and be less likely to run into anyone on his way down.

As he emerged from the stairwell, Colin glanced left then right, trying to think like a man running from a murder scene.

To the right was the front entrance to the hospital, with people coming in and possible security cameras pointed in that direction.

He turned left and followed the exit signs for that direction. Hurrying through the hallways, he imagined the murderer walking fast, but not necessarily running. Running would draw too much attention. Since he'd commandeered a food trolley to hide his moves until he'd reached the deputy, he was smart enough to know he had to blend in.

A nurse in scrubs passed him.

Colin stopped her. "Did you see a guy wearing scrubs pass through here in the past few minutes?"

She smirked. "I've seen a dozen."

"One with a goatee?"

The smirk left her face, replaced by a frown. "Actually, yes." She rubbed her shoulder. "He bumped into me and didn't even say an excuse me or kiss my ass."

"Which way did he go?"

She pointed. "That way."

Colin slipped past the nurse and raced down the hallway.

"If you catch up to him, you can tell him to kiss my ass," the nurse called out behind him.

If he caught up with him, he'd do a lot more than that.

Following the exit signs, he burst through an exterior door into a back parking lot labeled STAFF ONLY.

He looked around. At first, he didn't see any movement. Then he saw a dark sedan pull out of a parking space so fast the tires spun on the pavement before getting traction and shooting the vehicle forward. The driver glanced over his shoulder.

If Colin wasn't mistaken, the man had a goatee, and he was wearing scrubs.

Colin ran after the sedan, hoping to catch a glimpse of the license plate. And he did. But only the last three characters. BSH. He pulled out his cellphone and called 911.

After the dispatcher answered, Colin said. "This is Colin McKinnon. There's been a murder at the hospital."

"Sir, that has already been reported," the dispatcher said.

"Good. I'm calling because a dark sedan just left the parking lot. It might be the man who committed the crime. I only caught the last three characters on the license plate—BSH. He turned north out of the parking lot. If there are any units in the vicinity, they need to stop him."

"Thank you for the information. We'll handle it from here," the dispatcher assured him.

Sirens wailed, the sound growing louder as Bozeman police units drew closer.

Colin turned back to the hospital. When he tried the door he'd exited, it was locked from the inside. He had to go around to the front entrance to get inside.

Bypassing the elevator, he took the stairs up the few flights to the floor where he'd left Emily and the sheriff.

Several Bozeman police officers emerged from

the elevator at the same time as Colin came out of the stairwell.

Emily and Sheriff Barron were talking with the doctor who'd taken over from the nurses.

When Emily saw Colin, she hurried over to him.

"Were they able to revive him?" Colin asked.

She shook her head.

"Cause of death?" he asked, his gaze on the sheriff who was speaking to the doctor.

"Strangulation."

"He was a loose end," Colin said.

Emily's brow puckered. "Loose end?"

"Whoever wanted you out of the picture didn't want to leave someone behind who could be questioned."

Emily's eyes widened. "So, they killed their own guy?"

"That would be my guess." Colin nodded toward the sheriff. "Give me a minute with the sheriff, then I'll be ready to go to the bank with you."

She nodded.

Colin waded through the hospital staff to get to Sheriff Barron. "Sir, I called in a partial license plate of someone I saw peel out of the parking lot a few minutes ago."

"Thanks. I spoke with the Bozeman PD. They're looking for him."

"Emily and I are headed to the bank. Let us know if you need anything."

"Will you be in Bozeman long?" the sheriff asked.

Before Colin could answer, a rumbling boom shook the hospital.

Everyone grew silent.

Colin's gaze met Emily's.

"What the hell was that?" Sheriff Barron muttered.

In the next second, the Bozeman police officers' radios all went off at the same time.

In the chaos, Colin overheard one of the officers say, "Blew up the bank? You've got to be kidding."

The officers ran for the elevator. Some hit the stairwell and ran down to the ground floor.

"Did you hear that?" Emily hurried over to where Colin stood beside the sheriff.

"I did. One of the officers said something about the bank being blown up." He had a bad feeling.

"You think it was Alex's bank?" Emily asked. She turned to Sheriff Barron.

He was on his cellphone, speaking to someone on the other end of the call. His gaze met hers and shifted to Colin. "Thanks. Let me know if I can help." He ended the call and faced Colin and Emily. "What bank was it you were supposed to go to?"

Emily gave him the name and the address.

The sheriff let out a low whistle. "Someone really doesn't want you two to let Alex's cat out of the bag."

"Was it his bank?" Emily asked.

Colin knew the answer before the sheriff nodded his head.

"Someone entered the bank a few minutes ago,

asked to see the vault with the intention of securing a safe deposit box. When he left, he apparently left a present in the vault. The entire vault and everything in it were destroyed, along with half the block. It's a disaster area. They don't know how many bank employees or customers were killed in the blast. They haven't been able to get into the rubble yet to find any survivors."

"Holy hell," Emily muttered, pressing her knuckles to her mouth.

Colin leaned close. "This is not your fault."

"This has got to stop," she murmured. "People are dying because of what Alex knew."

"Yeah. Let's just hope that the destruction of the vault will satisfy them. Otherwise, we can count on them coming after you again." He was even more worried than he'd been the night before. These people were determined to keep their secrets safe from discovery, no matter who they had to kill to make that happen.

CHAPTER 7

EMILY'S HAND shook as she reached for the door handle on Colin's truck.

Colin covered her hand with his. His big body hovered over hers, a veritable shield against any bullets that might fly her way.

"How did my life come to this?" she asked, her voice catching on a sob. "People are dying all around me."

"This is happening because of what Alex did, and the people involved don't want it to get out. It's nothing to do with you, other than the fact Alex left his legacy for you to deal with. If he weren't already dead, I'd be tempted to kill him myself." His voice was harsh, filled with anger, and his fingers tightened around hers.

"He can't get any deader," Emily pointed out, her tone flat. "Whatever he's done is done. I have to figure out how to convince the people trying to clean up the loose end of Alex that I don't know anything. They've successfully destroyed our only chance of revealing who might be behind his death, the attempt to burn down my house and now the destruction of the bank."

"These people are dangerous," Colin said. "You can't stay in your home. They will be back. And this time, they won't fail at destroying the house and everything and everyone in it.

Emily knew he was right. She didn't want to leave her home, but she wanted to live. "I can't go to my sister's house. If they want me dead, they'll look there next." She climbed up into the truck and sat with her hands twisting in her lap. What would she do? Where could she go that was safe for her, as well as the people she cared for most?

Colin rounded the front of the truck and slipped in behind the steering wheel. "You can stay at the Iron Horse Ranch. We have a security system in place, and my brothers will help make sure you're safe."

"They're all busy looking for your father." Emily's frown deepened. "And you should be looking as well."

"I am searching for him. And I plan on doing more as soon as we settle the matter of where you'll be staying. As for that matter, your sister needs to stay at the Iron Horse, too."

Emily didn't like being beholden to anyone, but she wanted her sister to be safe. If it meant staying at the Iron Horse Ranch, so be it. "I have no problem with that. But Brenna will not be happy. She won't want to leave her little house. After all the work she's put into it remodeling it, she'll want to stay and defend her property."

Colin's lips twisted into a wry grin. "Sounds like something Brenna would do." He started the engine. "You'll just have to convince her it's the right thing to do. She can replace *things*. You can't replace *her*."

Emily nodded, her heart squeezing hard in her chest. "Brenna is my last family member alive. I don't know what I'd do if something happened to her."

"Then it's settled," Colin said. "You two are moving onto the Iron Horse Ranch."

Emily's lips twisted into a grin. "Don't you think you should check with your family? Shouldn't they have a say?"

"I know my mother. She'd be the first to load you and your belongings into a truck and haul you out there. And she'll probably kick me out of my old room and give it to you and Brenna." The corners of his lips quirked.

Emily's smile widened. "Your mother would give the shirt off her back to help others." Her smile faded. "I pray they find your father soon. And alive."

Colin's lips tightened. "Me, too." His cellphone rang before he could place the gear into drive. He didn't usually answer phone calls from numbers he didn't recognize. Usually, the unknown callers were telemarketers trying to sell him siding for a house he didn't own or get him to sign up for insurance he didn't need.

But with all that had happened in the past couple of weeks, he didn't dare ignore a call.

He accepted the call and pressed his cellphone to his ear. "Yeah."

"Hey, this is Buddy from the Bozeman pawnshop," a gruff voice spoke into Colin's ear. "Is this the guy looking for that woman with the unicorn tattoo?"

His pulse quickening, Colin answered, "Yes, it is. Did she come back?"

"Not only is she back, she's still here," the man said. "I stalled her by telling her I had to check with my partner about the price for a ring she brought in. If you want to catch her, you better be here in the next two or three minutes."

"I'll be there. Keep her there." Colin dropped his cellphone into the cup holder and shifted the truck into drive.

"Who was that?" Emily asked.

"Pawnshop owner. He's got the girl with the unicorn tattoo in his shop. Right now."

"You better hurry before she leaves. Is the shop very far from here?" Emily leaned forward.

"It's in a little strip mall a few blocks away." Colin pressed his foot down hard on the accelerator, shooting the truck forward.

Emily held onto the armrest and prayed they would get there before the woman left. She could be the key to finding Colin's father.

Colin took a corner so fast the back end of the truck fishtailed sideways, almost sending the vehicle into a spin.

He held tightly to the steering wheel, righting the truck and pushing forward as fast as he could go until he took the next corner. This time, he slowed before he entered the turn, taking it in a more controlled manner. He wanted to get there, but he was smart enough to know it would take longer if they spun out and wrecked.

Emily sat back in her seat, wondering what this woman with the unicorn tattoo could know that might lead them to John McKinnon. If she had pawned the ring he'd been wearing when he disappeared, she had to know something. If not where he was, she would know who had given it to her. Yet another clue to follow. It was more than Colin and his family had to go on since he and his brothers had come home.

Moments later, he came to an abrupt halt in front of a pawnshop.

Several bicycles were lined up in front of the building, along with a portable generator, lawn mower and a chainsaw. The windows were covered in iron bars making it hard to see inside to know if the woman was still in the shop.

As soon as Colin slammed the shift into park, Emily unclipped her seatbelt and slid from the passenger seat to the ground.

"You should wait for me," Colin said.

"I told you before, I don't want you using your body as a human shield to keep bullets from hitting me by letting them hit you first." She raised a hand and patted his cheek. "I'll be okay," she said.

He captured her hand in his and raised it to his lips. "Sweetheart, I hope so. And I'll be here to make sure you remain okay."

They entered the shop together, Colin cupping Emily's elbow, still shielding her body with his.

She didn't like it, but for the sake of expedience, she didn't fight him.

Inside, the pawn shop owner stood behind the counter, his attention on the woman in front of him. She had a shock of badly bleached blond hair and wore a pair of blue jeans two sizes too small for her curvy figure. Her top wasn't much more than a swatch of material barely covering her breasts and exposing a lot of her midriff. She had a hot-pink sweatshirt tied around her hips and a pair of sandals on her feet.

"I won't take less than fifty for the ring. It was my grandmother's wedding ring. I know that's at least a 2-carat diamond stone. My gran told me granddaddy had to work two jobs to pay for that ring."

"I'm sorry, miss," the shop owner was saying. "That's all I can do." He waved toward the glass cabinet beneath his hands. "I have a dozen diamond rings. They ain't worth anything if they don't sell. And they don't sell. Thirty-five. Take it or leave it."

She snorted. "Fine. I'll take it. But I'll be back next

week when I get paid to get it back. My granny would roll over in her grave if she knew I was hawking her wedding ring."

"Then maybe you shouldn't," the shop owner said.

"A girl's gotta eat, don't she?" the woman said.

The shop owner glanced over her shoulder at Colin and Emily. "I'll be right with you." He counted out thirty-five dollars and exchanged the money for the ring.

The blonde wadded the bills into a tight roll and slipped it into the front of her shirt as she turned toward the door.

That's when Emily noticed the unicorn tattoo on the inside of her forearm.

Colin must have just noticed it as well. His body stiffened, and he dropped his hold on Emily's arm. "Excuse me, ma'am, could I have a word with you?"

The blonde quickly stuffed the roll of bills into her bra and straightened, her nose tipping upward. "I ain't got time." She started to walk around Colin.

He stepped in front of her. "We need to talk."

Her eyes narrowed. "You ain't some undercover cop, are you?" She shot a glance from him to Emily and back to the man behind the counter. "Buddy, you didn't call the cops, did you?"

"Don't know what you're talking about, Missy." The shop owner unlocked the glass cabinet and slipped the ring inside. Just as quickly, he closed the door and locked it again.

Missy propped a fist on her hip and tilted her

chin. "What do you want? And make it quick. My boyfriend's waitin' for me to get back."

"I want to know where you got the men's ring you brought in over a week ago. The one with the inscription inside," Colin asked, his voice tight, his stance stiff.

Her eyes shifted slightly before she said. "I don't know what you're talking about." She tried to step around Colin only to bump into Emily.

Emily gave her a tight smile. "We know you sold the ring to this pawn shop. I understand the need for money, and we're not trying to take any away from you." Emily softened her voice. "It's just that the ring means a lot to us. The owner of that ring means a lot to us. We need to know where you got it?"

Missy's brow furrowed. She glanced from Emily to Colin and back. "I didn't steal it."

Emily touched the woman's arm. "No, of course you didn't. Please. It's okay."

Missy chewed on her bottom lip. "He'll kill me if I tell you. He don't like it when people come askin' him questions."

"Who, Missy?" Emily urged, her voice, low, insistent but gentle.

Missy glanced past Emily and Colin toward the door. "I gotta go. He'll be waiting. If I don't get back with the groceries, he'll…well, he won't be nice."

"Are you afraid of him?" Emily asked.

"Damn right, I am." She shifted from one foot to the other. "He busted my nose once. Just because I couldn't find his damned cellphone fast enough." She touched the bump on the ridge of her nose.

"Do you need help getting out of a situation, Missy?" Emily reached out her hand to the woman.

Missy stared at the hand, her eyebrows forming a V. "No one can help me. If I run, he'll find me. I'd better get back before he comes looking." She edged her way around Colin.

This time, he didn't block her path.

"Missy," Emily called out as the blonde reached the door. "Who gave you the ring?"

The blonde shot a glance back over her shoulder. "Same one who busted my nose. Now, leave me alone. I wanna live to see another day." With that parting comment, she left the building, turned left and walked quickly away.

Emily wanted to run after her. "We can't let her go back to him."

"We can't stop her. She didn't give us a name, but we can follow her and see where she ends up." Colin reached for Emily's hand.

She didn't hesitate. Placing her hand in his, she hurried toward the door. Missy was in an abusive relationship. She hadn't given them the name of the man who abused her, but hopefully, it wouldn't take long to figure it out. And once they did, they might be on their way to finding Colin's father.

Emily's heart raced as they left the pawn shop. She searched the sidewalks and streets for Missy, but the woman had disappeared.

CHAPTER 8

"Damn," Colin cursed. "She can't have gotten away that fast." He turned the direction Missy had gone and trotted to the next corner.

Emily kept up with him, without any problem. "See her?"

He shook his head. "No." He scanned the immediate vicinity, turning in a three-hundred-sixty-degree circle.

"Wait." Emily pointed down the alley. "Did the brake lights blink on that car?"

Colin glanced in the direction Emily pointed.

At that moment, the brake lights came on and blinked off again. The older model Ford sedan pulled away from the side of a building and drove toward the opposite end of the alley from where Emily and Colin stood.

"That has to be her," Emily said.

"Stay here, close to the building, but in the shadows. And keep an eye on her as long as you can," Colin said. "I'll be right back."

"Where are you going?" she asked.

"To get the truck." He ran back to the pawn shop, jumped into his truck and raced back to the corner where Emily waited.

She hopped up into the truck and leaned forward. "Hurry and we might catch up to her."

"Which way?" Colin asked, his foot shifting from the brake to the accelerator.

Emily tilted her head to the side. "South."

Colin hit the gas, sending the truck lurching forward on the main street through the center of Eagle Rock.

"There," Emily said, leaning forward. "She turned left three blocks ahead."

"She's headed out of town."

"How will you follow her without her knowing?"

"We'll hang back enough that hopefully, she won't notice." Colin sped up to the intersection and turned left. The vehicle he'd seen in the alley was about a quarter of a mile ahead, picking up speed.

Colin pressed hard on the accelerator, pushing the truck faster, but not so much that they caught up with Missy.

Two miles out of Eagle Rock, Missy turned onto a dirt road that led to an old trailer park. Colin knew about it because one of the members of his high school football team had lived there.

The bus Colin and his brothers rode to school

stopped there on the highway to pick up the kids from the trailer park. On good weather days, the boy either rode his bicycle to town and back or jogged in. That kid had been in the best shape of any of them.

Milo Morgan had gone on to play football on a full scholarship for the University of Montana Grizzlies. It took him five years, but he earned a degree in engineering before he went on to play in the NFL.

"You remember Milo?" Emily asked into the silence.

Colin nodded. "I was just thinking about him. He ended up doing well for himself, didn't he?"

Emily nodded. "He's working for an architectural firm in Bozeman. I think he landed the design work for rebuilding that old resort north of Eagle Rock."

"Good to see him doing well. He had a tough beginning."

"He was the most determined young man in town."

"He didn't want to end up in that trailer park all his life." Colin drove past the turn-off.

"Aren't we going to see which trailer she went into?" Emily twisted in her seat, looking back at the road they'd just passed.

"We will," Colin assured her. He drove several yards further along the highway, found another dirt road that appeared to have been forgotten. He pulled off and drove into the underbrush, parking his truck beneath a tree.

"I need you to stay in the truck while I go check

out where Missy went." He leaned across Emily's lap, opened the glove box and pulled out a pistol. "You know how to use this. Hold onto it in case someone discovers your location while I'm out nosing around."

"No way," Emily said. "I'm not sitting here while you're walking into danger. For all you know, her boyfriend could be a crack addict or murderer." She shook her head. "I'm going with you."

"You're the target in this situation. If he is a murderer, he could be the one who has already tried to kill you. I can't let you walk into his cross hairs."

"Colin, honey," she said, giving him her best teacher-talking-to-the-dense-student look, "you don't have to *let* me do anything. I have a mind of my own, and I can do anything I want."

Colin's brow descended. "I might not be able to keep you safe."

"You're wasting your time and breath." She unbuckled her seatbelt and dropped down out of the truck. "I'm going to find Missy."

Colin pressed his lips together. When Emily got an idea into her head, she could be just as stubborn as he was. He wouldn't talk her out of going with him.

"Well, hold onto that pistol and only use it if your life is in danger."

"Got it." She started for the road.

"Nope." Colin gripped her elbow and steered her through the woods. "The idea of hiding the truck in the woods was so that we could sneak up on the trailer park and recon the situation before moving in."

"Right," Emily said. "I knew that." She turned back toward the woods.

Colin took the lead, forging a path through the brush to the trailer park that consisted of twenty single-wide mobile homes in varying stages of disrepair.

The park might have been nicer a couple of decades before, but no one seemed to care anymore if there was trash piled up around the units, or old vehicles sitting on blocks, rust taking over where paint and metal had been eaten away by rock salt from too many harsh winters.

From the safety of the tree line, Colin and Emily studied the trailers, moving past one after the other until they reached the last two trailers in the park.

Since it was still the middle of the day and during the work week, Colin didn't expect there to be many people around. But there were more than he'd thought.

A grizzled old man sat on a ramshackle wooden porch, smoking a cigarette, a can of beer in his other hand.

At another trailer, he could hear the sound of a baby crying. A woman yelled inside that she was coming and soon the baby stopped crying.

At the last trailer in the far corner of the trailer park, Emily gasped, pointed and stepped backward, deeper into the shadows. "That's the car."

With nothing but woods behind the trailer, the location gave Colin and Emily the opportunity to get closer without being seen.

They eased through the forest and around to the back of the single-wide mobile home with siding that had seen better days. Dents, rust and mildew covered the faded tan panels. The unit had a front door with a small wooden deck that appeared to be dangerously ramshackle. Parts of the railing and the steps had rotted through.

The back of the trailer was even more nondescript than the front with a single door and a set of stairs that had probably come with the trailer made of metal angle iron and wooden planks that were gray and weather-worn.

A male's voice sounded from inside the trailer. He sounded angry and he was shouting.

Something smashed against a wall accompanied by the sound of glass shattering.

"You think Missy is okay?" Emily gnawed on her bottom lip, her brow furrowing. "She was afraid her boyfriend wouldn't be happy that she'd taken too long getting back to him."

"I don't know," Colin said. "We'll listen and see if it gets worse. Couples have arguments all the time."

"Yeah, but they aren't always accompanied by throwing and breaking things," Emily said.

Colin nodded. "True."

The next moment, something else hit the wall. It didn't sound like a cup, a glass or a plate shattering. It was more like something heavy slamming into a wall. Like maybe a person.

"I don't feel good about this," Emily said.

"Let's get closer," Colin stepped out of the shadows and moved toward the back of the trailer, without putting himself in view of a window, in case one of the occupants of the trailer just happened to glance outside.

Emily went with him.

The nearer they moved, the more they could make out the voices of the people inside and the words they were shouting at each other.

"I told you not to go back to Buddy. He's robbing you blind. I can't believe you traded your grandmother's wedding ring. That was stupid."

"We had to have money to buy food to eat for the week."

"What's wrong with the venison in the freezer?"

"It's been there for a year. I doubt it's any good."

"Why the hell didn't you use it? That's good meat. And you wasted it."

"I don't know how to cook venison. I don't even like it."

"You'll like it if it's the only thing we have to eat," the man yelled.

"We'd eat better if we had more money coming in."

"Can't you get more hours at the tavern?"

"Why, you'll just piss away all my tip money on

beer," Missy said. "When was the last time you had a job?"

"God damn it, woman. I told you I'm working on something. I don't need some dumb bitch nagging me about getting a job." A sharp clapping sound rang out and a loud thump followed.

"Get up, bitch."

"Please, Roy. Don't hit me. Last time you broke one of my ribs. I'm just getting over that."

"You should have thought of that before you started nagging me."

"Please…" Missy sobbed, her voice carrying through the thin walls of the trailer. "Don't."

Colin shook his head. "I can't stand back and do nothing."

Emily nodded. "Me either."

He stared down into her eyes. "I need you to stay here." Before she could protest, he held up his hand. "If Missy's boyfriend is involved in my father's disappearance or in the attempted arson or murder, I can't be worried about you. Please. Just stay."

Emily frowned, but nodded. "Okay. But don't do anything that will get you shot."

He grinned and held up two fingers. "I promise. Scout's honor."

Emily smirked. "You were never a scout."

"No, but I read the manuals." His lips twitched.

"Doesn't count." She turned him around and gave him a gentle push. "Don't get yourself killed."

Though her voice was flippant, he could sense the

deeper meaning and truth in her tone. Emily really didn't want him to die. She'd lost too many of the people she'd loved.

Colin rounded the trailer to the front and picked his way up rotted steps to the equally rickety porch and knocked on the door.

The shouting inside ceased. Heavy footsteps sounded on their way across the floor of the trailer.

The next moment, the door flung open and a man with dark hair, dark eyes and scraggly goatee stared out at him with a heavy frown. "What do you want?"

"Are you Roy?" he asked.

"Yeah. What's it to you?"

"I'm Colin McKinnon," he said. "I need to ask you some questions."

The sudden flare of recognition in the other man's face gave him away.

"Heard of me?" Colin asked, his jaw tightening.

"No," Roy said and tried to slam the door in Colin's face.

Colin stuck his boot in the crack and winced when the door smashed into it. Thankfully his boot kept his foot from being crushed.

"Get off my property," Roy demanded.

"I might…." Colin said in his deepest, most threatening tone, "after you answer some questions for me."

"I don't know nothin' about your father."

"Who said I was going to ask about him? But since you brought him up…" Colin grabbed Roy by his collar and lifted him up several inches, pulling him out of the trailer onto the wobbling porch. "Where's my father, John McKinnon?"

Roy clawed at the hands holding him up. "How should I know?"

"Apparently, you know something. You gave his ring to Missy. Where'd you get the ring, if not off my father's finger?"

"I don't want no trouble," Missy cried. "Let him go."

Colin glanced over Roy's shoulder to Missy.

The woman had emerged from the trailer with a bruised cheek and tangled hair. She held a pistol in her shaking hands, aiming it at Colin and Roy.

"Put down the gun, Missy," Colin said. "This bastard isn't going to hit you again."

"I'm not worried about him hitting me. I had it coming. But if you hurt my Roy, I'll...I'll...shoot you." She gripped the weapon tighter.

"Missy, put down the gun," Emily said from the bottom of the steps. "Put it down and nobody gets hurt."

"He's going to kill my Roy," Missy said, her eyes wide.

"Colin isn't going to kill Roy," Emily said. "We just want to know where you two got John McKinnon's ring."

"He'll kill him," Missy said, tears streaming down her cheeks. "Let him go. Please."

"I'm not going to kill this abusive sack of bull

crap," Colin said. "But I'm not letting go until he tells me where he got my father's ring."

"That's just it," Missy said. "If Roy tells you where he got it, the guy he got it from will kill him."

"What guy?" Colin lifted Roy higher off his feet, his arm straining. "You better start talking." Without turning, he said, "Emily, get Sheriff Barron on the phone."

"No!" Missy cried, her hand jerked, and the gun went off.

Roy grunted and grew slack in Colin's grip.

Emily raced up the stairs, grabbed Missy's hand and shoved it upward, away from the two men standing so close.

Colin didn't have much choice but to guide Roy's body as he slumped to the ground. He couldn't hold up the dead weight of the man.

"Roy!" Missy released her hold on the gun.

Emily secured it and hurried down the steps, away from Missy and Roy. As soon as she was on the ground, she pulled her cellphone out of her pocket and hit three keys, dialing 911.

Colin squatted beside the downed man.

Roy lay on the weathered wood porch, clutching his side where blood spread across his shirt. "God damn woman should have left well enough alone."

"Oh, baby, I'm sorry." Missy dropped to her knees beside him. I didn't mean to shoot you."

"At least you got me before he did."

"Who?" Colin demanded. "Who would kill you?"

Roy lay back, closing his eyes. "I don't know. He wore a mask."

"Why did he wear a mask?" Emily asked.

"I guess because he didn't want me to know who was paying me to burn down your house."

"Bastard," Colin said through gritted teeth.

Roy coughed. "Man's gotta make a living, whatever way he can."

"Did he pay you to kill the man in the hospital?"

"He paid me to leave no loose ends."

"Roy, baby, why did you agree to it?" Missy asked.

"We needed the money. And I had a feeling that if I turned him down, he'd have killed me on the spot." He shrugged and winced. "Seemed like I didn't have a choice. Do it or die."

Emily's brow furrowed. "Did he say why he wanted you to burn down my house and kill me?"

Roy harrumphed and coughed for his effort. "I asked. He said, *'Just do it.'*"

"Did he give you the ring?" Colin asked.

Roy snorted and coughed. "Hell, no. I lifted it from his pocket. He never knew I took it." Roy glared at Missy. "And he wouldn't have known I got it, if Missy hadn't taken it to the pawn shop."

"How was I supposed to know you stole that ring?" she cried. "Oh, God, you're bleeding everywhere." Missy leaped to her feet and ran back into the trailer, returning with a hand towel. She folded the towel into a square, shoved Roy's hand aside and pressed the square of material against the open wound.

Emily turned away and spoke into her cellphone, giving the 911 dispatcher the nature of her emergency and location. When she was finished, she faced Colin. "Ambulance and police are on their way."

He didn't have much time

"Was there anything about this man that you stuck out? Could you see his hair color, or the color of his eyes? Did he wear something that was unusual?"

Roy's eyes blinked, and his face grew paler. "I don't know. It was dark outside the tavern. He handed me a wad of cash...told me that he'd kill me if left any loose ends. Now that you know what I know...just leave me alone," Roy said. "If this bullet didn't do me in, I know another one will. I'm a loose end."

Colin didn't say it, but he thought Roy deserved to die after killing his partner in crime. But mostly, he deserved a painful death for attempting to kill Emily by burning down her house with her in it, and then trying to shoot her.

The wail of sirens sounded from the direction of Eagle Rock. Before long, two sheriffs' vehicles arrived, followed by a first responder fire truck and an ambulance.

Colin hooked Emily's arm and led her away from the action.

Sheriff Barron joined them. "I take it from the

way Missy was carrying on, you weren't the one to shoot Roy," the sheriff said.

"It wasn't me, though I wish it had been. The man's dangerous and will do anything for the money."

The sheriff pulled out his pen and pad of paper from the front pocket of his uniform. "I don't suppose you got a confession out of him."

Colin nodded. "He was the one who killed his partner in the hospital."

"I heard him, too," Emily said. "And he and his partner were the ones who tried to burn down my house and shot at us."

"Did he say why he did that?" the sheriff asked.

Colin's lips pressed together, and he clenched his hands into fists. "Someone paid him to do it."

"Did you get a name?"

"No," Colin said. "He said the guy wore a mask and paid him in cash outside of the tavern."

"I'll question him at the hospital, if he survives until then."

"You might want to have more than one guard watching him," Colin suggested.

The sheriff's mouth twisted. "Already thought of that. You two need to watch your backs. If someone was willing to pay Roy to kill Miss Emily, he might be willing to pay some other miscreant to finish the job."

Colin grinned. "Already thought of that. She'll be

staying out at the Iron Horse Ranch until this gets resolved."

Sheriff Barron nodded. "Good idea. But remember, you can't always hole up at the ranch. If you do have to venture out, make sure she has a bodyguard."

"Will do," Colin said, gathering Emily into the curve of his arm. "If you don't need us for anything else, we're headed to the ranch."

"If I have any more questions, I know where you live." The sheriff clapped a hand on Colin's shoulder.

Colin led Emily out of the woods and walked along the road back to where he'd stashed the truck.

When he pulled out of the dirt road onto the highway, he started to turn right.

"Where are you going?" Emily asked.

"I told you...to the Iron Horse Ranch. You're staying with us until this threat is neutralized."

She smiled. "I'm willing to go to the ranch, but I'll need clothes and toiletries from my house before I go out there. I can't go with just the shirt on my back."

Colin gave her a sheepish grin. "Sorry. I didn't think about that."

"And your go bag is at my place. You might need that. We also need to collect my sister. That might take some doing." Emily chewed on her bottom lip, making Colin want to lean over and kiss her.

Colin winked and turned toward Eagle Rock. "Leave her to me. I know how to work her."

Emily chuckled. "You do, do you?"

Colin liked the sound of her laugh. "We have to

get past all this. You need to laugh more. I always loved your laugh."

Hell, he'd always loved Emily. He just hadn't known how much until he'd kissed her behind the barn. By then, it had been too late. He'd committed to the military, and she'd wanted stability.

Had coming home to Iron Horse Ranch been two-fold? To find his father and to have a second chance at a life with the only woman he'd ever loved?

CHAPTER 9

ON THE DRIVE back to Eagle Rock, Emily pulled out her cellphone and called her sister, Brenna.

"Hey, sis," Brenna answered. "I heard you had some trouble at your house last night. Just to let you know, I heard it from a waitress at the diner."

Emily cringed at the accusing tone in her sister's voice. "I'm sorry. I should've called you immediately. It's just that the past twenty-four hours have been insane."

"Yeah, I might have lost my sister and wouldn't have known until it was too late," her sister's voice dripped sarcasm. "I'm on my way to your place to perform an intervention. It appears your Marine isn't taking good enough care of you, since he's letting people try to burn down your house."

"He didn't let anyone try to burn down my house. I'm glad he was there, because he put out the fire and chased one of them down. Otherwise, my house would've been nothing but ashes with me inside, burned to a crisp. And the arsonists would have gotten away with the crime."

Her sister didn't answer immediately. When she did, her voice was calmer. "Okay. I guess I'll cut him some slack. But I'm still coming over to your place. I want to see for myself that you're okay."

"Sweetie, before you come, pack yourself a bag with enough clothing and toiletries to last at least a week."

"Are we going on a trip?" Brenna asked.

"Something like that. I'll explain when you get to my place. See you soon."

"You bet you will," Brenna said.

Emily ended the call and shot a glance toward Colin. "She'll be over in less than fifteen minutes."

"That fast?"

"She lives on the other end of town, and Eagle Rock isn't that big."

"Yeah, but she still has to pack a bag."

"And curiosity for why she might need one will be killing her." Emily grinned. "I give her fifteen minutes. That should be enough time for me to pack one of my own."

Colin drove into town and turned onto the street where Emily's house stood. The house was on the very edge of town, far enough away from her nearest neighbor she could have screamed her head off and no one would have heard from inside their well-insulated homes.

Emily shivered. She'd loved that they had so much space around the house. It had been a beautiful, quiet little retreat. A great place to raise children.

Now, all she could think of was the isolation. She really did owe Colin her life. If he hadn't been there with her, she might have been severely injured or killed.

Before she could open the car door, Colin laid a hand on her arm. "Stay in the vehicle while I check the grounds."

Emily didn't argue. The Marine had combat experience. He knew what he was doing.

He started with a wide sweep of the yard, ducking into the trees and behind bushes, searching for anyone who might be lurking.

When he emerged after making a complete circle around the house, he climbed the steps to the porch and reached for the doorknob.

Colin hesitated, his hand halfway to the knob. With a quick glance back at Emily sitting in the car, he stood back from the door and nudged it with his foot.

The door swung open without him having to turn the knob.

Emily leaned forward. "What the heck?" She reached for the handle on the car door. Had the house already been opened? She had been certain she'd shut the door and locked it before they'd left that morning.

She reached for the pistol in the glove box and pushed open the car door.

Even armed, she didn't feel any safer. Not with Colin inside, possibly facing another paid killer. He hadn't come back out yet, and he didn't have a backup.

Emily hurried toward the front door, the pistol in her hand, aimed forward. With every step she took, she reminded herself, *think before you shoot.*

She didn't want to shoot Colin, mistaking him for a bad guy.

Tiptoeing up the steps, she eased across the porch and pushed through the front door.

Her first thought was that she'd entered the wrong house or a post-apocalyptic war zone. This couldn't be her house. Not the clean, neatly organized space she'd made her home for the past eight years.

The table beside the door had been smashed into firewood. The brown leather couch Alex had insisted on purchasing had been slashed into pieces, the stuffing ripped out and strewn all over the floor. Every cushioned chair had been ripped to shreds, including the padded seats around the dining table.

The television lay on the floor, the plastic casing shattered. The television stand's doors had been broken off, the side drawers pulled free, the contents flung throughout the room.

"I'm sorry, Emily," Colin said from the stairway

up to the second floor. "The only good news is that whoever did this, isn't here."

"The bedrooms?"

He shook his head. "Equally destroyed."

"Why?" she asked, shaking her head, unable to process the devastation.

"Since every drawer and cushion in the house was torn into, I'd say they might have been looking for something."

"The ledger Alex talked about was stored in the safe deposit box in the bank." She stared up at Colin as he descended the staircase. "They destroyed the bank. What did they think they'd find here? Surely, I would have found anything Alex might have left here. I've been through all his effects. I found nothing."

"Perhaps he hid it so that you wouldn't find it. Or the people who had this done think Alex might have more information hiding in his house. Information you might not know exists." Colin crossed the floor, stepping over broken furniture and puffs of cushion stuffing.

When he reached her, he pulled her into his arms and held her.

Emily rested her cheek against his chest, listening to the reassuring beat of his heart. The sound reminded her that he was still alive. And she was still alive. That was what was important. Things could be replaced.

"Is there anything left in my room? Do I need to bother packing a bag?"

"The clothing in the bedroom where you slept is there. Not in the closet. I don't think they slashed them like they did the couch and chairs.

"I'd better pack a bag. It's very clear to me I can't stay here." She pushed away from Colin's embrace and started up the stairs toward the room she'd slept in since her falling out with Alex.

She peered into the master suite and the other bedroom before stepping into her room. Her clothes had been yanked from the closet so hard the rail had come loose and lay bent and broken on the floor, along with her blouses, dresses and trousers. Every pair of shoes had been pulled off the shelves and flung across the room. The mattress was in shreds, pushed from the frame, the box springs torn beyond any chance of repair.

Her gaze shot to the top of the dresser where she'd kept her jewelry box. The box wasn't there.

Emily dug through the piles of clothing, the bedding and mattress stuffing, frantically searching for the little wooden jewelry box, the only thing she'd kept of her mother's belongings. In it was her mother's diamond engagement ring that her father had given her when he'd asked her to marry him.

Her mother had loved that ring and everything it stood for. She'd made Emily promise not to bury it with her. It was the only thing of value she had to leave to her oldest daughter.

By the time her mother had passed away, she'd already removed the ring and placed it in the jewelry box her mother had given her. She'd been too thin to wear the ring and too afraid it would fall off and she'd lose it.

Emily couldn't lose the ring. It was all she had left of her mother besides memories.

Tears slipped from her eyes as she pushed through her damaged belongings in search of her past.

Colin knelt on the floor beside her. "What are you looking for?"

"My mother's jewel box. I have to find it." When she didn't find the box beneath her clothing, she moved to where the mattress had been pushed off the side of the bed and tried to lift it back into place. On her knees, she couldn't get the leverage she needed to move the mattress back onto the boxed springs.

"Let me," Colin said. He rose to his feet, grabbed the edge of the mattress and swung it over to lie in its proper place.

Emily pawed through the bed linens and the comforter until her hand fell upon a hard object beneath all the fabric. She yanked the comforter aside. Lying on the floor was the jewel box her mother had left for her, broken into several pieces.

Gathering all the pieces into her lap, Emily sifted through the bracelets, earrings and necklaces until she finally found the diamond solitaire ring. Clutching it to her chest, she let the tears fall.

When her mother had died, she'd held her grief inside. As the oldest and only person left, besides

Brenna, she'd felt she had to be strong for her little sister.

She'd stood dry-eyed beside the casket when Alex had been laid to rest, the horror of losing him and her unborn baby still too fresh in her mind for her to digest and comprehend.

Somehow, in the disaster of her house, the dam burst, and all the tears she hadn't shed burst free and fell, drenching her face, her hands and her clothes.

Colin lifted her to her feet. "I can fix the box," he said. "Please, Emily, don't cry. I can fix it."

"You can't," she cried. "I don't care about the house, the furniture, the years I've lived here. They don't matter. You can't fix this, Colin." She shook her head, the tears running down her face. "You can't bring back my father or my mother. You can't bring back Alex, and you can't bring back the baby I lost in the crash. Those things can't be fixed."

"You're right," he said. "But you still have Brenna. And me. We're still here. You aren't going to lose us."

She stared up at him through her tear-soaked eyes. "How do you know? You're a Marine. Doesn't that make you a target for enemy bullets?"

"Em, you can't borrow trouble. It's no way to live. You have to appreciate what you have, when you have it. You're not guaranteed tomorrow. If you spend all of your life worrying about things that are out of your control, you'll miss all the good stuff."

"I know you're right. But it's hard to see past all that's happened. I'm beginning to think it's me. I'm the jinx. I keep losing the people I care about. I'm afraid."

He pulled her into his arms and held her close. "It's okay to be afraid, as long as you don't let it stop you from living. Courage is not the absence of fear, but the triumph over it." He smiled as he pushed aside a damp tendril of her hair. "Who said that?"

"Nelson Mandela," Emily said, her tears drying.

"If anyone had a crappy life, he did. But he didn't give up." Colin tipped her chin up. "And neither will you."

She nodded and sniffed noisily. "I know. But I'm allowed at least one meltdown along the way."

Colin grinned and kissed the tip of her wet nose. "That's my Em. Now, go wash your face before your sister gets here, or she'll blame me for making you cry." He winked and turned her toward the bathroom in the hallway.

As he walked behind her, the floorboard beneath his foot creaked loudly.

Colin frowned and pushed the bedsheets aside to stare down at the wooden flooring.

Emily shook her head. "That board has been squeaking for the past year. I meant to have someone fix it but never got around to it."

Colin leaned down and ran his hand across the slat and picked at it with his fingernail.

The board popped up, revealing a hidden compartment beneath the floor.

"What's this?" He bent and slipped his fingers into

the compartment. A moment later, three more floor-boards slipped out of place. Beneath them lay a short metal box.

Colin drew the box out of its niche and set it beside the hole in the floor. "Maybe this was what they were looking for."

Emily's eyes rounded. "I've been stepping on that squeaky floorboard for so long, it didn't even occur to me that it was a hiding place." Her brows twisted. "I swear I didn't even know Alex near the end. He kept so many secrets."

"He probably didn't want you to get wrapped up in what he was doing."

"And keeping secrets was his way of protecting me?" She snorted. "That's bullshit."

"I can't really speak for Alex. All I know is this box might give us a clue as to who he was dealing with." Colin tried the latch. It didn't budge. "It takes a key."

"Well, that key might've been lost with Alex—or was blown up in the bank vault explosion. The key he left in the package was definitely a safety deposit box key." Emily glanced around. "I'll be right back."

She ran from the room, hurried down the stairs and returned moments later with the hammer they'd kept in the kitchen. Granted, she'd found it on the floor along with the contents of her small tool bag Alex had gifted her with on her birthday.

She held out the hammer. "You want to do the honors, or shall I?"

He took the hammer with a smile. "I'll do it. You look mad enough to destroy everything in that box."

"I think I have a right to be angry. I didn't sign up for this crap, but here we are." She waved a hand at the mess.

Colin turned the box over a couple of times. Whatever was inside rattled with each turn. Finally, he laid it on the floor and banged the locking mechanism twice with the hammer. On the second tap, the box bounced open.

Inside was an older model cellphone, the kind that flipped open.

Colin opened it. "The battery is dead." He looked inside the box again, but it was empty. He replaced the slats in the floor, covering the hiding place and then asked, "Did Alex keep charging cables somewhere?"

"In the nightstand in the master bedroom," Emily jumped up and led the way to Alex's nightstand. She hadn't made the effort to go through all of his things yet. She just hadn't felt like it. After losing him and the baby, she'd walked around in a fog for weeks. And since she wasn't using that bedroom, clearing out the room hadn't made her priority list for dealing with it anytime soon. The top drawer had been full of books, cards and old letters, which were now strewn across the room. The bottom drawer, a neatly arranged storage place for what seemed like every electrical gadget cord imaginable, had miraculously remained untouched.

Colin had followed her into the room. He turned the phone upside down and stared at the shape of the plug. Then one by one, he held up charging cords until he found one that fit the phone. He tested it in the electrical socket next to the bed and a green light blinked awake on the cellphone.

He unplugged the cable and slipped it into his jacket pocket. "We'll charge it at the ranch. Your sister will be arriving soon, and you don't want her to walk into this mess without a little warning."

"No, I don't want her walking into this. She'll freak out." Emily was halfway to the bedroom door when she heard Brenna's voice downstairs.

"Emily?" A split second later, her sister called out, "What the hell? Emily!"

"I'm okay," she said, hurrying to the top of the stairs.

Brenna stood in the front entrance, her hand on the doorknob, her face white. "Oh, thank God." She hurried toward her, picking her way through the mess.

Emily descended the stairs and hugged her sister.

"I don't understand," Brenna said. "What the hell, Sis? Tell me you weren't here when... this...happened."

"We were in Bozeman," Emily reassured her.

"Why would someone do this to your house?"

"We think they were looking for something," Colin said as he came down the stairs to join them.

"You can't stay here," Brenna said. "It's not safe."

Emily nodded. "Agreed." She glanced over her shoulder at Colin. "I'm going to stay at the Iron Horse Ranch until things settle down."

Brenna grimaced. "I'd offer to let you stay with me, but I'm not so sure that'll be safe either. Someone has it out for you."

Emily took her sister's hand. "You need to come stay with me at the Iron Horse Ranch."

Brenna's eyebrows rose. "Is that why you had me pack a bag?" She snorted. "And here I thought we were going on a spontaneous vacation." Brenna shook her head. "I'll be fine at my place. I just had all the locks reworked, and I have a .40 caliber pistol I can keep handy."

Colin and Emily shook their heads at the same time.

"If someone wants to get to Emily," Colin said, "he might use whatever means is necessary to get to her."

"Including you," Emily added.

"Exactly." Colin slipped an arm around Emily's waist. "You and I both know that Em will do anything to keep you safe. If someone kidnaps you, Emily will move heaven and earth to get you back."

Emily nodded. "I'd trade my life for yours."

Brenna was shaking her head. "You can't do that. Your life is just as important as mine."

"You know she'd do it," Colin said. "If you don't go with her to the Iron Horse Ranch, you're setting yourself up as a target to get Emily to come out into the open."

Emily squeezed her sister's hand. "I won't rest unless I know you're safe." She pressed Brenna's hand to her cheek. "You're the only family I have left."

Brenna cupped Emily's face in her hand. "Anything to keep you safe. You're the only family I have. We have to stick together." She glanced up at Colin. "Fine. I'll go with you. But I still have a job. How am I supposed to do it from the ranch?"

Colin grinned. "We'll work on that. I have some friends I can call in to help."

"I hope your friends like showing houses. I can't make money if I'm not showing houses. That's what we real estate agents do." She blew out a long breath. "Well, looks like we are going on a spontaneous vacation. I just didn't expect it to be so close to home and on a ranch. You know I don't do horses, right?" Brenna winked.

"You won't have to," Emily said.

"Good. You were the one who liked riding across the fields with the wind in your hair."

"And you were the one who preferred to stay home and read books and magazines about home design." Emily hugged her sister. "I'm glad you're coming with me."

"I'm glad I'm going with you, too." Brenna squeezed her hard, and then leaned back and smiled into Emily's eyes. "Seems I can't leave you alone for a minute without something horrible happening to you." She looked around. "Need help packing a bag?"

"As a matter of fact, I do." Emily led the way up the stairs with Brenna in tow.

"I'll keep watch from down here," Colin said. "Don't worry about me. I'm just part of the furniture."

"Oh, quit being a baby," Brenna called out, chuckling.

Emily laughed, her heart a little lighter now that her sister was near. She prayed Brenna wouldn't become collateral damage in whatever game these people were playing against her.

COLIN PLACED a call to Sheriff Barron, reporting the vandalism to Emily's house and letting him know they would be heading out to Iron Horse Ranch as soon as they'd packed what they needed to stay for a while.

"I'll have my team out there to investigate as soon as possible," the sheriff said. "I'm glad you're taking the ladies out to the ranch. With all your brothers there, they ought to be safer than if they stayed home."

"That's the idea," Colin said. "What's the word on Roy?"

"Roy Keats is in bad shape. The bullet nicked some vital organs. They were taking him into surgery when I left the hospital. The Bozeman Police Department has two officers guarding the surgical floor. They've got strict orders to keep a really close eye on Roy. After what happened earlier today, they'll be on their toes."

Colin didn't tell the sheriff about the phone he'd found in the floor of Emily's house. Though he trusted the sheriff, he figured the fewer people who knew about it, the better off Emily would be. And talking over the phone wasn't necessarily a secure means of communication.

After he ended the call to the sheriff, he placed one to the ranch, letting them know they would have two visitors staying indefinitely.

His mother assured him she wouldn't have it any other way. She loved Emily and Brenna like daughters, and they could stay as long as they needed.

Emily and Brenna came down the stairs, each carrying a suitcase.

"We're ready," Emily said.

"I'll follow you in my car. I don't like to be dependent on anyone for transportation, especially if I need to get somewhere quickly," Brenna said.

"Tell you what," Colin said. "We'll follow you out to the ranch. "That way, we have your back."

"And who will have yours?" Brenna asked, one eyebrow raised.

Emily grinned. "I have a gun. I'll keep an eye to the rear in case we run into any more trouble."

"That's what I like," Colin said. "Teamwork."

Brenna climbed into her car and pulled out of the driveway.

Emily and Colin followed in the truck.

The drive out to Iron Horse Ranch went without a hitch. When they arrived at the house, his mother and his sister, Molly, came out on the porch to greet them.

"Where are Duncan, Angus and 'Bastian?" he asked.

"Your brothers are out in the canyon again. I don't know what they hope to find, but they were pretty determined to get out of the house and do something," his mother said. She smiled at Emily and Brenna, taking one of the suitcases out of Emily's hands. "Let me have that. Colin says you've been through hell the past couple of days."

Molly reached for Brenna's case. "Let me show you to the room we arranged for you two. You'll be sharing a room since we have all the boys home."

"I can carry my own case," Brenna said. "But thanks. It's enough you're putting us up. Hopefully, it won't be for long."

"Thank you, Mrs. McKinnon." Emily hugged the older woman. "You don't know how much we appreciate your kindness. I'm so sorry to hear about your husband. I hope they find him soon."

Colin's mother gave Emily a tight smile. "They will. We just have to believe he's still out there and waiting for us to find him and bring him home."

She didn't say it, but Colin filled in the rest of the sentiment.

Alive.

They had to believe they would find him and bring him home alive.

Once they were inside the house, Colin took the case from his mother and from Brenna, despite her protest, and carried them up the stairs.

Molly led the way to room on the other side of Colin's. "Duncan's been staying in town with Fiona and Baby Caity. Emily and Brenna will be staying in his old room." She opened the door and stood back, letting Colin enter to set down the suitcases.

Emily slipped in after him and set her smaller case on the queen-sized bed. "Thank you. This will work great. We don't want to put you out too much. Brenna and I can help with the cooking and cleaning. We don't expect to be waited on."

"That's good, because I'm a terrible cook, and I'd rather be out mucking stalls than running a vacuum." Molly grinned. "I would have thought you'd rather be out riding horses than being stuck inside, Emily. I remember you, Colin and Alex out here practically every day during the summer." She frowned. "You only took me along with you when Mama made you." She glared at her brother. "Some big brother."

"You were a pain in the butt, little kid. And we did take you along on our picnics." He grabbed his sister around the neck and rubbed his knuckles across the top of her head, like he had when they were much younger.

"Hey, I'm not ten anymore," Molly said, pushing away from Colin and smoothing her hands over her hair. She turned her attention to Emily and Brenna. "Don't let him bully you. He can be as big a pain in the butt as he claims I was." She dodged Colin's reach and dove for the door. "It'll be nice to have more females around for a while. I'm always outnumbered. Dinner's at six."

"I'll be down to help with it," Emily said. "Thanks, Molly."

Molly disappeared down the stairs, leaving Emily and Brenna with Colin.

"I'll leave you two to get settled in." Colin backed out of the room.

Emily followed him. "Let me know when you get that phone charged enough to look at it." She spoke in hushed tones.

"Will do. I'll be in my father's office. It might be best to keep its existence between you and me. Whoever tossed your place might have been looking for it. If they know we have it, they might come out here looking for it."

"Should we turn it over to the sheriff?"

"We will—after we've had a chance to look at what's on it."

She nodded. "I'll be down in a few minutes."

Colin took her hand and brought it to his lips. "I'm glad you're here. I feel much better knowing you'll be surrounded by people who will look after you."

"You and your family are so generous. I don't want to get in the way of your search for your father."

"You're not," he said. "I'm still working on that. I get the feeling Alex's associations and what's happened to my father might be connected. I don't know how yet, but I think it's worth looking into."

He didn't want to let go of her hand. Hell, he wanted to take her into his arms and kiss her. But they had work to do. The phone had to be a clue as to what Alex had been up to. Or rather who he'd done business with. The sooner they discovered who that was, the sooner they might find Colin's father.

Yeah, he might be grasping at straws and doing a lot of wishful thinking but, like his mother had said, they had to believe they'd find his father. If that meant reading more into a situation than might be there, so be it. Lately, in his search for his father, he'd begun to lose hope. Grasping at straws gave him a small amount of hope.

CHAPTER 10

EMILY UNPACKED a few of her things and hung them up in the closet next to a few items of Duncan's clothes. She was careful to leave room for Brenna, as they would be sharing the room for who knew how long. The rest of her things, she left in her suitcases. If they stayed longer than a few days, she'd unpack more.

Anxious to help and not be a burden to a family who was already going through their own problems, she hurried downstairs to the kitchen.

She knew her way around the house. She'd been there so many times while growing up that she could find her way in the dark, if she had to.

Colin's mother, Hannah McKinnon, stood at the stove, stirring something in a large stockpot.

"Can I help?" Emily asked.

"Sure. I never turn down an extra pair of hands.

I'd forgotten how much food it took to feed all my boys."

"I remember sitting down to dinner with your clan on more than one occasion." Emily chuckled. "It was a lot of food."

"They burned a lot of energy," Mrs. McKinnon said. "Thank goodness we raised our own beef. And my vegetable garden came in handy."

"If I remember correctly, you had a pretty big garden. Colin, Alex and I swiped a couple of watermelons from it over the course of a several summers. I'm just sorry we didn't clear it with you first."

"I knew you were taking them. That's why I grew them. Although, I would have liked a piece." She winked and nodded toward a recipe card on the counter beside her. "I'm making Colin's favorite, chicken and dumplings. You can make the dumplings. I usually double the recipe amounts for the dumplings."

Emily followed the recipe, mixing flour, shortening and chicken broth to make the pastry. Then she rolled it out on a pastry sheet until it was less than a quarter of an inch thick.

Mrs. McKinnon handed her a pizza cutter to cut the dumplings into inch-wide strips.

"The soup is ready when you are." Colin's mother stepped away from the pot she'd been stirring.

Emily dropped the dumplings in, a handful at a time. When they were all transferred from the pastry sheet to the pot, she cleaned the sheet and rinsed the flour from her hands.

"You made those like a pro." Mrs. McKinnon beamed at her.

"I've done it a few times. Alex remembered how much he loved your chicken and dumplings whenever we ate over here. I learned how to make them like you do." Emily shrugged. "That was as good an excuse as I needed. I loved them, too."

"Comfort food," Mrs. McKinnon said. "I figured we could all use a little comfort food right about now."

Emily nodded. "I can't imagine how you're holding up. Not knowing is somehow worse than bad news."

Colin's mother gave her a weak smile and went back to stirring the dumplings. "I'm going with the no news is good news way of thinking. And I'm keeping busy.

"That was some kind of how-do-you-do in Bozeman last night. I can't believe someone slammed your car into the side of that building." She shot a worried glance toward Emily. "I don't know what's wrong with people. I'm just glad you weren't hurt."

"I was glad Colin was there. I'm not sure what I would've done if he hadn't been."

"No kidding. Especially since you were attacked in your own home after the shenanigans in Bozeman." Mrs. McKinnon pulled her spoon out of the stockpot for a moment. "I'd be afraid to breathe.

You're not safe out of your house, and you're not safe in it."

"That's why I'm here," Emily said. "Thank you for making your home available to me and Brenna."

"Honey, you're family. I'm glad you came." She gave Emily a crooked grin. "There was a time I thought you and Colin would end up together." She shrugged. "Not that I'm trying my hand at match-making or anything. It's just that you two had so much in common."

"All three of us did. We were the Three Muske-teers," Colin said from the door to the kitchen. "Can I steal your assistant chef for a few minutes?"

His mother smiled at her son. "Of course. She was just showing me how to make dumplings."

"I'm sure you already know how."

"I do. But it's fun when someone else spends time with me in the kitchen." His mother nodded toward the door. "Don't worry about me. You've done the hard part. All I have to do now is make sure it doesn't burn to the bottom of the pot."

Emily followed Colin out of the kitchen, her pulse beating a little faster and a swarm of butterflies beating against her hollow belly. All because Colin had probably overheard his mother talking about them being together.

She wouldn't have been so jittery if the same thought hadn't crossed her mind on more than one occasion in the past twenty-four hours.

What would have happened if she'd followed her heart and married Colin instead of Alex?

With that thought came a sad one. If she'd married Colin, Alex might be alive today. He wouldn't have felt compelled to take on highly lucrative work for dangerous people.

That thought slowed her pulse and put a damper on the butterflies in her belly.

Colin led her into his father's study where he'd left the cellphone charging on his father's desk.

"Apparently, Alex had a passcode on this phone. Any idea of what he might have used?"

Emily shook her head. "Did you try his birthday?"

Colin nodded. "I tried a few variations of the day, month and year. None of them worked."

"Mine?"

Again, Colin nodded. "I tried combinations, forward and backward of both of your birthdays."

"Wedding anniversary?" she suggested.

"Tried it."

"His mother's birthday?"

"Don't know that one."

She gave him the date.

Colin tried multiple combinations of the date, to no avail. He finally shook his head. "We could spend a lot of time guessing. But I have a friend with resources who might be able to hack into the phone and download all the data."

Emily frowned. "That's letting more people in on the fact we have the phone."

"These people can be trusted, and their facility is secure."

Emily chewed on her bottom lip. "If you think it's okay, I'm okay with it. I want to know what's on that phone."

"Me, too." He lifted the phone on his father's desk and punched in a number. "Hank, I have a challenge for you and your team." He paused to listen. "I can't discuss it over the telephone. I'd like to drop by the White Oak Ranch and run it by you." Another pause. "Okay. I'll see you in a couple hours." He hung up and met Emily's gaze. "Hank Patterson is a former Navy SEAL. He started a security service called the Brotherhood Protectors. I've heard his computer guy is really good at hacking into just about anything. If he's as good as they say, he should be able to hack into this old phone."

"A phone is different than a computer," Emily pointed out.

"Yeah, but it's worth a shot."

"Agreed. I'd like to go with you."

Colin glanced out the window. "I hadn't planned on leaving until after supper."

"That's okay. I can wait."

"Good, because the chicken and dumplings smell good, and I'm starving."

"Because we didn't have lunch." She smiled. "Come on. We can help set the table."

Brenna joined them in the dining room. Between the four of them, they set the table, transferred the chicken and dumplings to a soup tureen and carried crackers, cheese and a fresh green salad to the table.

Minutes later, Duncan, Angus and Sebastian clomped up on the porch.

Sebastian leaned through the back door to the kitchen. "Something smells good."

"Chicken and dumplings," his mother called out. "Wash up. It's on the table."

The men pulled off their boots and walked through the house to the first-floor bathroom, jockeying for position in front of the sink to wash their hands and faces.

By the time they settled in their chairs, Mrs. McKinnon and Emily had set glasses of water in front of each plate at the long table.

Molly burst through the back door. "Sorry. I got caught up mucking a stall and lost track of time."

Sebastian shook his head. "You're the only girl I know who could miss supper because she's shoveling horse sh—"

"'Bastian," his mother cut him off. "No cursing at the table."

"Mom, I'm not fifteen anymore."

Emily hid a grin.

Sebastian was over six feet tall, broad-shouldered and built like a tank. The man had been through hell and back in Navy SEAL training and had been deployed many times. But his mother still held power over him.

"All the more reason to set a good example," she said, her tone stern.

"Yes, ma'am." He turned to Molly. "Shoveling horse poo."

His brothers howled with laughter.

"Shut it," Sebastian warned with a glare.

"You could all clean up your language while you're home," Mrs. McKinnon said. "There are ladies present."

"Molly doesn't count," Sebastian said. "And Emily's one of us."

"That leaves me and Brenna," his mother pointed out. "And I beg to differ when it comes to Emily and Molly. They're both lovely young ladies. So, mind your manners."

"Yes, ma'am," Sebastian said, his brow creased in a deep frown.

Again, his brothers roared with laughter.

The meal went along with the men poking fun and goading each other and Molly jumping in whenever she could throw a barb or two.

Emily felt comfortable enough to join in on occasion. It was as if the ten years hadn't passed, and they were all still the kids she'd known from high school.

Only the boys had become men. They'd gone off to war, fought battles, watched men die. And she'd stayed in Eagle Rock, married to a man she loved as a friend, because she had been afraid of loving a man who could have ended up dying on a battlefield.

Emily stared around the table at the men who'd seen death and could still laugh. They'd come home to find a father who might not be alive. But they put on a brave front for the mother and sister they loved. They were family.

They didn't stop loving each other when they were afraid. They powered through and held each other up when they were down.

A lump lodged in Emily's throat, making it impossible to swallow. She forced food down in tiny bites. Thankfully, the chicken and dumplings went down easily, and she was able to finish the meal without gagging.

When Mrs. McKinnon rose to start clearing the table, Emily jumped up to help.

"Oh, no," Mrs. McKinnon held up a hand. "Emily helped cook. Brenna and Colin set the table. That leaves Molly, Sebastian, Duncan and Angus to clear the table and do the dishes."

Despite the matriarch's edict, Emily still carried her plate to the sink and rinsed it.

"I've got this," Molly said. "You and Colin have better things to do."

"But you hate household chores," Emily protested.

"Hate is a strong word. Dislike? Now, that's more my speed. I dislike going to the dentist, but I do it because it needs to be done." She gave Emily a broad smile. "I do the dishes, because it needs to be done."

Sebastian twisted a towel and popped Molly's backside. "And I'm here to help."

"That's not helping." Molly glared at her brother. "Act your age, little man. As Mother said, there are ladies present."

Brenna carried her plate to the sink. "Don't change on my account. I can take care of myself. And I've heard all the curse words."

Colin draped an arm around his younger brother's shoulders. "'Bastian, seeing as you don't have a clue how to act around women, how about spending some time with one."

Sebastian perked up. "You know one?"

Colin nodded. "As a matter of fact, I do." He turned to Brenna. "Brenna needs a bodyguard when she leaves the ranch."

The younger brother frowned. "Bodyguard? I had more interesting things in mind."

Colin explained the situation to his brother.

Sebastian raised an eyebrow. "Can't say that I've ever pulled bodyguard duty. I'm more of a blow and go kind of combatant."

"Seriously. I don't need a bodyguard," Brenna insisted. "I can manage on my own."

Emily frowned. "If you're showing houses, you're alone and vulnerable."

"I've been doing it for two years. I think I know how to handle situations," Brenna said.

"Yeah, but things are different now." Emily couldn't stress enough how dangerous it would be. "Someone is after me. If they think they can get to me through you, they will."

"I'll take my chances," Brenna said, her lips pressed into a prim line.

"Sorry, Brenna, I can't let a little lady like you wander around the county unaccompanied." Sebastian puffed out his chest. "Since my brother has enlightened me as to the seriousness of the tasking, I have to agree with him and Emily. You're not safe. And if you're not safe, Emily isn't safe." He grinned. "I'll be your bodyguard until further notice."

"What about your father?" Brenna asked. "Shouldn't you be searching for him?"

"I can do that while helping you out," Sebastian said. "When you're in town, I can ask questions and follow up on leads. And maybe when we're out looking at land and houses, I might see something, like an abandoned shack where they could be holding my father hostage."

"Now, there's a thought," Angus, Colin's oldest brother, said. "Going around the county with a real estate agent might be just what we need. If our father is being held hostage, it very well could be in an abandoned house or hunting cabin. Maybe we've been looking in the wrong place."

"Yeah," Duncan picked up the line of thinking. "Maybe Hank Patterson has a drone we can borrow, or we can hire someone he can recommend who operates one."

"I'm headed over to Patterson's place now. I'll ask him."

"Why are you going to see Patterson?" Angus asked.

Emily bit down on her bottom lip. She and Colin had decided the fewer people who knew about the phone, the better. But they hadn't planned to out and out lie to his brothers.

"I want to see if he has any other ideas," Colin said. "Maybe his team of Brotherhood Protectors has seen something in their various duties. I don't know what he'll suggest, if anything. But it doesn't hurt to ask."

Emily's lips quirked at the corners. She swallowed a smile.

Colin hadn't exactly lied. He just hadn't told his brothers the whole truth. Their trip to see Hank would serve dual purposes—continue their search for their father and find a way to hack into the cellphone Alex had hidden in the floor of their house.

Colin turned to Emily. "Ready?"

"Wouldn't you rather one of us went with you?" Angus asked.

Colin waggled his eyebrows. "As much as I appreciate your company, Emily is prettier. And I promised to keep an eye on her."

"She'll be fine here on the ranch with all of us here to keep her safe," Duncan pointed out.

"Again, I appreciate the offer, but I kinda would like to spend a little alone time with Emily." He shook his head. "And you made me spell it out when I didn't want to be so obvious."

Duncan raised his hands in surrender. "Sorry, man. Didn't realize you were taking Emily on a date. I didn't know it was that way between the two of you."

"It isn't," Emily assured the brothers, though her cheeks heated, and she had to look guilty. Not that she had anything to feel guilty about.

Colin was putting on a show to convince his brothers that he wanted to be alone with her. It was all fake. He only wanted to be alone with her, so they didn't have to reveal the fact they had a cellphone they wanted Hank's computer guy to hack into.

Emily hated lying to his family. The sooner they found out what was on that phone, the sooner they could share it with the rest of his family, and they wouldn't have to keep secrets.

Secrets had been what got Alex killed and might be what would get her killed as well.

"I'm ready when you are," Emily said. She looped her arm through Colin's and smiled at his family. "Don't wait up on us. We might be late."

Sebastian whistled. "Don't do anything I wouldn't do."

"Which leaves just about anything open to possibilities," Molly said, her lips twisting. "Be careful out there. If someone is out to get you, they could be waiting for you to leave the ranch to make their move."

"We'll be on the lookout," Colin assured Molly. "Thanks for caring."

"I just want you to bring Emily back safe. She makes some mean dumplings, and we can always use a backup in case Mama goes on a cooking strike." She winked and looped her arm around her mother's shoulders.

"Don't tempt me," Mrs. McKinnon said. "Now, go on, get out of here. The sooner you get there, the sooner you get back, and I can quit worrying about you two."

Emily left the house, still holding onto Colin's arm. She didn't let go until they reached the passenger side of his truck, and he opened the door. Truth was, she didn't want to let go. She liked holding his thickly muscled arm. She wondered what it would feel like to be held so close to his body that they could feel the beat of each other's heart.

He'd changed a lot since he'd left to join the Marines. He must have grown another four inches since high school, and his muscles had thickened, his shoulders getting broader and his chest was as hard as stone.

A shiver rippled across her skin.

"Are you cold?" Colin asked as he handed her up into the truck.

Heat rose up her neck and into her cheeks. She was glad the sun had gone down and all the light shining on her face was from the inside of the truck, casting her in a shadow as she climbed up into the seat. "Maybe a little," she responded as she bent her head to buckle her seat and pull herself together.

Now wasn't the time to fall in love with her best friend. They had bigger issues to solve than affairs of the heart.

CHAPTER 11

HANK PATTERSON, former Navy SEAL, had already helped the McKinnon family through his team called the Brotherhood Protectors. The group of men were former special operations Marines, Navy SEALs, Army Delta Force and Rangers.

They'd helped when Duncan had troubles with the Faulkner clan when they'd kidnapped his baby girl.

One of Hank's men was a computer genius capable of hacking into databases with the tightest of firewalls and security systems. Surely, he could handle one older model cellphone.

Colin and Emily drove to the White Oak Ranch where Hank lived with his movie star wife, Sadie McClain, and their baby girl Emma.

At the gate, he hit the intercom button and looked up into the camera so that whoever was on the other side could clearly see who was driving the truck. "Colin McKinnon here to see Hank."

A moment later, the gate opened, and Colin drove through.

"I'm already impressed with Hank's electronics," Emily murmured.

"I understand he has all the latest in communications equipment and weapons. He could run his own army out this ranch, if he wanted."

"That's a lot of power."

"Yeah, but he's a good guy. He only wants to help people who can't help themselves. In the process of providing security services to others, he's giving former military men a place where they can best use the training they worked so hard to acquire. Most of the men he employs would have had a much harder transition into the civilian world without an organization like the Brotherhood Protectors to work for."

"I didn't even know they existed until today. It's nice to know they're so close to Eagle Rock." Emily tilted her head, appearing thoughtful. "Perhaps I could contract them to provide my protection."

Colin's jaw tightened. "I'm here for you."

"And I appreciate that you are," Emily said. "But you'll eventually have to return to your unit. And we don't know if that will be before or after we discover who is behind the attacks on me, my house and my husband."

Emily had a point.

Colin's lips thinned. He was on active duty. He

couldn't be gone from his post forever. And Emily had made it clear a long time ago that she had no desire to marry a military man. She'd never wanted to go through what her mother had when she'd lost her husband to war.

His heart squeezed tightly in his chest. He loved being a marine. He loved that he was part of something much bigger than himself. Defending his country, the people and their way of life was deeply ingrained in him.

Yet, he loved Emily. Always had. Could he give up his career in the military in order to stay in Eagle Rock with Emily? They'd only kissed. What if she wasn't as into him as he was into her? He could give up his military career and not win the girl. Then what? What kind of life could he lead back in Montana?

He could join forces with Angus, who'd given up his career in the Delta Force to remain in Montana to run the ranch, with their father, when he returned, or by himself, if he didn't. Angus would need help. The ranch had the capacity to expand its beef production. But that would require more people to help manage the animals, the feed and repairs to fences.

Colin thought about it. Now that he'd been away from home, he'd seen what the world had to offer. Would he be satisfied to remain in Montana for the rest of his life? And what about the work he'd done to earn his spot on the Marine Force Reconnaissance team? Was he willing to walk away from all that? For the love of a woman?

He shot a glance toward Emily. When he'd thought he could never have her, it had been easier to be away. Now that he was home and nothing stood in the way of him forging a new relationship with the woman, he really had to stop and think about it.

There was no doubt she was the one for him. But was he the one for her? Would she change her mind about being a military wife and, potentially, a military widow?

Not that Colin had any plans to die in the near future. But then, neither had Alex. And he hadn't been in the military.

Like he'd said, there were no guarantees in life. Death was the only guarantee. When it happened was unpredictable.

Would he give up everything he'd thought mattered to him to stay in Montana with Emily?

At that moment, she glanced across at him with those blue eyes he'd never forgotten.

Yes.

Eventually, he'd have to retire from the Marine Corps, anyway. He could see himself growing old with this woman, sitting in a rocking chair on a porch, overlooking the Crazy Mountains or a beach in Florida. It wouldn't matter to him, as long as he had her by his side to the end of his days.

Emily frowned. "What?"

"What?" he shot back, stalling.

"You were looking at me funny."

"I was just thinking you haven't changed since high school."

She snorted. "I've gained ten pounds, and I've got wrinkles showing up at the corners of my eyes."

"They add character."

"They make me look old."

"So, what's wrong with looking old?" He could imagine her blond hair turning gray, the crow's feet getting deeper, and she'd still be beautiful to him.

"Nothing, if you're a man," she said. "Women aren't allowed to grow old without someone making a big deal about it. Men just look more *distinguished*."

"We're lucky if we get to turn gray," he reminded her. "Even luckier if we get to know our grandchildren."

She glanced out the side window, apparently unaware her face reflected in the glass wearing a melancholy expression.

"Hey." Colin reached out and took her hand. "I'm sorry. I'm preaching to the choir. You of all people know about missing out on that kind of relationship."

Emily nodded. "My father would've been a really good grandfather," she said. "He loved kids. And my mother always wanted four or five grandchildren. She made me promise to have at least two. She said she'd keep an eye on them from Heaven." Her gaze went to where he held her hand. "Now, I'm thinking I'd be foolish to bring children into a world so dangerous."

"You can't let your current circumstances color the rest of your life." He squeezed her fingers gently. "This too shall pass, and Eagle Rock will once again be that safe, wonderful place to raise a family."

"Not for me," she said. "When I lost my baby, there was some damage to my female plumbing. The doctor said it would be highly unlikely I'd ever get pregnant again."

The hollowness in her voice hit Colin in the pit of his gut. Emily had always dreamed of having children. She'd wanted them to grow up with an appreciation for the simple things in life, like walking in the rain, riding a horse and petting a dog.

"I'm so sorry," Colin said. How did one console a woman who'd lost the most important function women alone could perform? Childbearing was a part of who she was.

Losing her baby had hit her hard. Losing her ability to have more…

Wow.

He had no words, but he had to try. "You know, being a mother isn't just about bearing children."

"I know. But I've always wanted children, of my own," she whispered.

His heart hurt for her.

Thankfully, they arrived at the ranch house.

Colin slowly rolled to a stop and shifted into park. "Need a minute?" he asked, not wanting to push her after revealing something as devastating as she had.

"No, I'm okay. I've had three months to learn to deal with my new normal. I'm almost over it."

"Almost." Colin snorted. "You're the strongest woman I know."

"I'm sure you've met stronger in the military."

He shrugged. "Physically solid, but you're every bit as strong, if not stronger than any one of them."

She gave him a weak smile, squeezed his hand and pulled hers free. "Thank you. Right now, I wish I was smart enough to figure out this phone. Hopefully, Hank's guy will do the job, and we'll get some answers."

A tall, brown-haired, green-eyed man stepped out on the porch, carrying a toddler girl in his arms. He smiled and waved at them as they climbed out of the truck and walked toward the porch.

A beautiful, petite woman with silky blond hair and baby blue eyes emerged behind him, a smile lighting her gorgeous face.

"I swear Sadie never ages," Emily murmured. "And she's as nice as she is beautiful."

Hank and Sadie stepped down off the porch and closed the distance to Colin and Emily.

"So glad you two came out together," Hank said. "Sadie was getting a little stir-crazy with mostly men to talk to lately. All the lady-folk have been busy working or visiting relatives."

"Oh, don't listen to him," Sadie said and pushed past Hank to extend a hand to Emily. "How are you? Hank tells me you've had some drama recently?"

Emily smiled. "I'm fine. Thankfully, none of my run-ins have resulted in injury to myself or Colin." She took Sadie's hand and shook it firmly. "My car, on the other hand, is toast. And my house is a war zone."

Sadie reached out and took Emily's hands. "Let me know when, and we'll help you set it to rights."

"Thank you." Emily pulled Sadie closer and hugged her, her eyes glistening. "You might regret offering."

"Never," Sadie said, leaning back to look into Emily's face. "We're a small community. We can't afford to avoid our neighbor's needs."

"Come in. Come in," Hank said, waving his free hand toward the house. "It's getting too cool out here for Emma. We can gather around the fireplace and warm up."

"By chance is your computer guy here?" Colin asked as they stepped into the living room.

"As a matter of fact, he is," Hank said. "I have him working on a project in the war room. Why?"

Colin pulled Alex's old cellphone from his pocket and held it out to Hank. "Think he could get past the passcode and find out what information is on it?"

"I'm sure he can." Hand stared down at the device and shook his head. "It's an older model. Where did you get it?"

Colin glanced across to Emily. "In a secret compartment hidden in the floor of Emily's house."

"We think Alex hid it there," Emily offered. "It

might contain information about the people who are trying to do me in." She chuckled. "Look at me sounding like mafia."

Colin slipped an arm around her waist. "I'm glad you can laugh about it. I'm having a hard time finding anything funny about someone trying to kill you."

Emily leaned into him, her body warm against his. "I probably wouldn't be so flippant if I didn't have someone like you watching my back."

"Let's go down to the war room." Hank handed Emma to his wife.

"Are you hungry?" Sadie asked.

"No, we just had dinner," Emily answered.

Sadie nodded. "Then, I'll make some coffee."

"Sounds perfect," Colin said. He was more interested in what was on the cellphone than the coffee, but he wouldn't pass up a cup.

Hank went to a wall at one end of the large living room and pressed his thumb to a bio-scanner. A moment later, a door slid open, revealing a staircase, leading downward into a basement.

Colin knew about Hank's bunker, but he'd never actually seen it.

He was impressed by the clean lines, the bright lighting and how big it was once they got to the bottom of the stairs.

The room was large with a conference table dead center, massive whiteboards on two of the walls and a couple of doors leading off the main room.

A man sat at a desk against the wall equipped with a six-monitor array. He glanced up and gave a brief nod of acknowledgement before he went back to work, typing madly on the computer keyboard.

Hank waited until the man was finished and turned to face him, before he spoke.

"Axel Svensen, this is Colin McKinnon and Emily Tremont."

"Call me Swede," the man said, his eyes narrowing. "You one of the McKinnon sons?"

Colin nodded.

"Sorry to hear about your father." Swede pushed to his feet and crossed the room to Colin, holding out his hand. "I know you must be beside yourself over his loss."

"We haven't given up on him, yet." Colin had to tip his head back in order to look the guy in the eyes. Swede had to be at least six feet six inches tall. He had white-blond hair and icy blue eyes. "Nice to meet you."

"Same." Swede tipped his head slightly and gave him a once-over glance. "Marine?"

Colin nodded. "How did you know?"

Swede's lips quirked upward on the corners. "Every Marine I've ever known has the corner on high-n-tight haircuts. Army, Air Force and Navy just can't get it as right as every Marine."

"And you?" Colin prompted.

Swede tilted his head toward Hank. "Navy SEAL, like Hank. We served together on one too many operations." His glance went from Hank to Colin and back. "Are you joining us on the Brotherhood Protectors team?"

Colin shook his head. "Not today." He looked toward Hank. "We heard you were a whiz at anything computer-related. How are you with hacking into cellphones?"

"I haven't actually done it, but that's never stopped me." He held out his hand.

Hank placed the phone in his palm.

"Whose is it?" Swede asked.

"Alex Tremont's," Colin replied.

Swede frowned. "I know that name. Wasn't he the guy who was shot in the head on his way home from Bozeman a few months back?"

Emily winced. "Yes. He was my husband." She held out her hand to the big SEAL.

"That would explain the same last name," Swede noted. "I'm sorry for your loss. Did they ever catch the shooter?"

"No," Emily said. "We hope this cellphone we found hidden in the floor of my house might give us a clue as to who might have done it."

"And who might be attacking Emily now," Colin added.

Swede's blond brow rose. "You're having troubles?"

Emily nodded.

"Well, let's get on this ASAP." Swede returned to his computer, set the cellphone on the desk beside him and fished in a drawer for a cable that would fit the phone with a USB port on the other end. Once he found one, he inserted the cable into the port and the USB connector into his computer.

For the next few minutes, his fingers flew over the computer keyboard.

Screens in the array flashed before finally bringing up a list of what appeared to be phone numbers.

"It'll take me some time going through all the numbers to find who they belong to," Swede said.

"How long?"

"I could have them to you by morning."

Emily's face fell, but she squared her shoulders and gave Swede a smile. "Thank you. Anything you can do will help."

"Anyone need some coffee?" Sadie descended the stairs with a tray filled with steaming coffee mugs.

"I could use some," Swede said.

"Allie called," Sadie said. "She said she misses you. I told her to pack a bag and come on over to stay the night. She should be here in thirty minutes."

Swede glanced up with a smile that lit his face. "Good. It's going to be a long night, and I miss my sweetheart."

"I told her I'd send one of the boys over to take care of the animals tomorrow."

"I'll take care of the animals tomorrow. Allie could use a break from dealing with our father," Hank said. "Since I've been back, Dad and I have a better understanding of each other than we did when I was a kid."

Sadie cupped her husband's cheek. "I love you, Hank Patterson."

"I love you, too." He quirked an eyebrow. "What did you do with Emma?"

"She got sleepy, so I bathed her and tucked her into her bed." She held up the baby monitor she'd clipped to her belt. "She's an amazing child, but I fear she's going to snore as badly as her father. I feel sorry for her future husband."

Hank frowned. "Husband? Please, Sadie. Don't marry off my daughter before I have a chance to teach her how to ride, rope and shoot. That way when she finds a man to love, she can leave if she's not happy, tie him up if he gives her grief, and shoot him if he causes her any trouble."

Sadie chuckled. "I get the feeling Emma won't have many dates."

"If I have anything to say about it, she won't. At least not until she's forty."

Sadie frowned.

"Okay," Hank said. "Maybe at thirty-five, but only if I can come along to make sure he doesn't try anything funny."

Colin liked their playful banter about their little girl. He wished he had as easy a relationship with Emily as Hank had with Sadie.

Hell, he wished he had a relationship with Emily, easy or not.

He finished his coffee and waited for Emily to finish hers.

"Hank and Sadie, thank you for your hospitality." Colin shook hands with Hank. When he held out a hand to Sadie, she brushed it aside and hugged him and then hugged Emily.

Colin grinned. "The boys back at the base will never believe I had coffee with Sadie McClain."

"You want to take a picture to prove it to them?" Sadie offered. "I don't mind."

"No. I won't do that to you. I figure Montana is your sanctuary where you can come be yourself. I can't even imagine what it's like to be hounded by the paparazzi and followed through the streets of L.A. whenever you're there. I see the photos and the clips on television. It has to be hard."

Sadie smiled. "I don't mind. I compartmentalize my life in L.A. I know it's my job as an actress to be available to my public. But when I come home to White Oak Ranch, I get to put all that aside and be the person I love most. And that's the mother of my child and a wife to my husband, whom I love dearly." She slipped her arm through Hank's and leaned into him. "I love our life together. "If my work as an actress dried up, I wouldn't be sad at all. I have everything I need here with Hank and Emma."

Colin nodded. "You're a lucky woman."

Sadie smiled up at Hank. "Yes, I am."

"Now, if you'll excuse us, we need to get back to the Iron Horse Ranch and leave you all to get some rest." Colin shot a glance toward Swede. "If you come up with anything odd or out of the ordinary, feel free to call me." He held up a hand. "No matter the hour."

"Wait." Hank ducked into back into the war room and emerged a minute later carrying a pendant on a silver chain. "I give these to all of the Brotherhood's ladies. It has a GPS tracking device embedded in the pendant. Wear it in case you get separated from Colin."

Emily smiled and thanked Hank. She slipped the necklace over her head and tucked it inside her shirt. "I hope we don't have to use it. But if we do, I'll feel better knowing I have a posse looking out for me."

Colin escorted Emily out to the truck and helped her up into the passenger seat.

She leaned back against the cushion and closed her eyes.

When Colin slipped into the driver's seat and cranked up the engine, he thought Emily had fallen asleep. He quietly backed away from the house, turned and drove down the long, sweeping drive. He didn't want to wake her.

Dark smudges circled her eyes. She looked tired. And who could blame her? Her world had been turned upside down with the death of her husband and her unborn child. And just when she had the chance to ease into her new life...bam! She'd nearly been killed. Not once, but multiple times.

"Do you think Hank and Sadie really do love each other as much as they appear to? Or do they put on a show to fool everyone into believing they're head over heels?" Emily asked without opening her eyes.

Her question made Colin frown. "Sadie might be a great actress, but I doubt Hank has an acting bone in his body. He loves her." Colin glanced her way. "Why would you think they don't love each other?"

"I don't know. It just seems too good to be true." Emily tipped her head toward him and peered at him through sleepy eyelids. "Is it possible to love someone that much?"

"I believe it is," Colin said, and meant it. Seeing Hank and Sadie together with Emma, their little girl, gave him hope that he would someday have that forever kind of love.

With Emily.

After being married to the wrong person, Emily would take some convincing that it was possible to love again.

Hope and determination swelled in Colin's chest. He'd learned from his father and mother that the best stuff was worth fighting for.

And Emily was the best stuff life was made of. If it meant giving up the Marine Corps, well then, maybe it was time to consider other career options.

Emily had closed her eyes again and appeared to be asleep as they passed through the night, headed back to Iron Horse Ranch.

Colin wanted her more than he'd wanted anyone in his life. So much so, that he felt almost a physical pain, tight in his chest.

When he pulled up to the house, and got out, he rounded the truck to the other side, with every intention of waging war on Emily's defenses.

He opened her door and helped her down, standing so close, her body slid down the front of his before her feet touched the ground.

"Hey there," he said, wrapping his arms around her. "Can you make it to the house, or do you need me to carry you in?"

She looked up into his eyes. "No one has ever carried me anywhere," she said. "Wouldn't be right to start now."

"Sometimes you have to embrace the adventure that is life," he said and bent to scoop her up into his arms.

Emily wrapped he arms around his neck and leaned her head against his chest. "Mmm...I could get used to this."

Colin could, too. He liked the way she felt in his arms. "It's a beautiful night. You want to sit on the porch for a while?"

She nodded. "As long as I don't have to move a single muscle." Emily snuggled into him and let him carry her up the stairs to the swing hanging on one end of the front porch.

He sat on the swing, settling her in his lap.

His mother leaned out the door and squinted toward them in the dark. "Is that you, Colin, or is it Sebastian?"

"It's me, Colin."

"Oh, okay. I thought Sebastian and Brenna might have gotten back by now."

Emily sat up straight in Colin's arms. "Brenna went somewhere this evening?"

"She did," Colin's mother said. "She had a phone call from a potential client who wanted to meet with her at the Blue Moose Tavern to discuss what he wanted in the way of land to build on."

Emily slid off Colin's lap and stood.

Colin's dream of snuggling with Emily and convincing her to give love a second chance, slipped away. He stood beside her.

"How long ago?" Emily asked, her voice tense.

"Right after you two left. I expected her to be back by now," his mother said.

Colin touched Emily's arm. "We can drive into town and make sure she's all right. I'd feel better if it was more than just you and me, but right now we don't have much of a choice."

"We'll be all right. I'm more worried about Brenna and Sebastian." Emily looked up at him, her eyes rounded and worried.

He swallowed a sigh for what might have been and nodded. "Let's go."

CHAPTER 12

EMILY'S HEART pounded against her ribs as she descended the porch steps and hurried toward Colin's truck. Brenna had gone out. At night. What had she been thinking?

Colin opened her door and waited for her to climb up inside.

Before she could put her foot on the running board, Mrs. McKinnon called out. "Oh, wait. I see headlights coming up the drive. That's probably them now. Brenna said to tell you that she wouldn't be too late."

Emily held her breath until a truck pulled up beside Colin's and Sebastian climbed down.

Before he could round the front of the hood, the passenger door opened, and Brenna hopped out. "Oh good, you're home. I almost had Sebastian drive me out to Hank's place to make sure you got back here safely."

"Did you have to go to town tonight?" Emily asked, her tone a little sharper than she'd intended, but the worry she'd felt made her snappy.

"I didn't know that I needed your permission to leave the ranch." She turned to Sebastian. "Besides, I made use of my own personal bodyguard and took Sebastian with me to give me backup."

Sebastian touched a finger to the brim of his cowboy hat. "For what it's worth, we didn't run into any trouble between here and there."

"Why would someone expect you to drop everything and run into town?" Emily led the way up to the porch, giving a brief glance to the swing she'd sat on a few moments before when she thought all was briefly right with her world.

She'd even considered snuggling with the man she'd always loved. For a moment, she'd let her walls crumble only to have her responsibilities rear up and slap her back to reality. She couldn't relax her guard for a moment.

What if the meeting Brenna had been called to had been a setup? A trap?

Emily's pulse beat faster.

"Hey, sis, relax." Brenna came to stand beside her on the porch. "You can't freak out every time I have to meet with a client. I'm a real estate agent. It's what I do."

Emily hugged her sister. "I can't help it. I love you and would do anything for you."

Brenna held her at arm's length, her lips firming.

"Which makes me your Achilles heel. I know. I wouldn't do anything to put myself in danger. You know that."

"I know that. But you're all I have left," she said, her voice catching on a sob. After swallowing hard, Emily squared her shoulders. "I'm sorry. I overreacted." She gave her sister a tight smile. "You're a grownup woman with a mind of your own. Sometimes, I forget."

Brenna chuckled. "And that's the mama in you. Even mamas have to let go of their chicks, eventually."

"Yeah," Emily said. "But not when the mama is being threatened, and whoever is threatening her might take advantage of her Achilles heel."

"Point made and taken," Brenna said. "But I did what you asked and took along my bodyguard." She touched Sebastian's arm. "He even looks the part, all buff and muscular." Brenna winked at Sebastian. "Thank you."

He tipped his hat. "My pleasure. Now, if you'll excuse me, I want to catch the rest of the game on television." Sebastian left the ladies standing on the porch and disappeared inside.

"I'm going to get a shower and wash my hair," Brenna said. "I'm showing Mr. Hunt some properties tomorrow and want to look my best. Hopefully, we'll find something he likes. The man appears to be loaded. He drives a Ferrari and wears a pretty swanky suit."

Emily chewed on her bottom lip. She wanted to forbid her sister from leaving Iron Horse Ranch, but she couldn't.

Brenna took her hand. "I see worry wrinkling your brow." She shook her head. "Don't worry. Sebastian vowed to be my bodyguard all day, if necessary."

Emily drew in a deep breath and let it out. "Okay. I guess it'll be okay. A man driving a Ferrari isn't likely to kidnap my baby sister. And if he did, a Ferrari will stick out like a sore thumb around here. We'll find it." She winked. "Don't hate me for worrying."

"I'd hate it if you didn't," Brenna assured her. "Good night, sweetie." She kissed Emily's cheek and entered the house.

"Now that everyone is where they should be, I'll be off to bed," Mrs. McKinnon said. "Be sure to turn off the porch light when you come in."

Mrs. McKinnon's departure left Emily alone with Colin.

Colin reached inside the house and switched off the porchlight. Then he took her hand and raised it to his lips. "I don't suppose we can pick up where we left off?"

Emily laid his palm against her cheek. "It's insane. Every time I'm around you, I lose focus."

"And that's a bad thing?"

She nodded and touched her lips to the inside of his hand. "We should call it a night. Tomorrow might be a busy day, depending on what Swede finds on that phone."

"Yeah." Colin drew her into his arms and pressed her against him. "You're right. We should call it a night."

A minute ago, Emily had been exhausted by the worry of not knowing where Brenna was. Now, in Colin's arms, adrenaline shot through her veins, revitalizing her senses.

This was the man she'd always been in love with. She'd settled for Alex because she'd been too afraid to love a man who would put his life in danger on a battlefield.

God, she'd been a fool.

When Colin bent to claim her lips, the ten years they'd been apart faded away.

This was where her heart belonged. In Colin's arms.

His mouth came down on hers, claiming her. His tongue traced the seam of her lips.

Emily opened to him.

He swept in, caressing her tongue with his in a long, sensuous twist.

Her hands found their way around his neck, pulling him closer until she didn't know where he ended, and she began.

The lights in the hallway blinked out, leaving only the stars to shine down on them, bathing them in a soft blue light.

When Colin finally broke away, he stared down

at her, his eyes reflecting the starlight. "I've wanted to do that for a very long time," he said, his voice husky.

"I've wanted it, too."

"What are we going to do about us, Emily?" Colin pressed a kiss to her forehead. "Where do we go from here?"

She shook her head, her thoughts in a haze of desire. "Well, we can't go to my room. Brenna's in there."

His stilled, his fingers gripping her hips, curling into her flesh. He tipped his head to the side. "Am I reading you right? Maybe you should spell it out for this Marine, so I don't make a mistake."

She leaned up on her toes, touched his mouth with hers and whispered, "Let's go to bed. Your room. Now."

It was crazy. She'd never come on to a man like this before. And she might regret it in the morning. But at that moment, all she could think about was getting naked with this man. "Don't think too much. Don't take it past the moment. I need to feel, to touch, to hold you."

Colin hesitated for a second. "Are you sure?"

She bit his bottom lip lightly. "I told you not to think. Don't ruin the moment. I want this. For now."

He swept her up in his arms and hurried toward the door.

Emily reached for the doorknob and whispered, "What about your mother?"

"I'm a grown man," he said. "And now, you're thinking too much."

She pulled open the door.

Colin carried her across the threshold and straight up the stairs. He passed the room she shared with her sister and stopped in front of his bedroom door.

Emily could have called a halt to the insanity at that point. Instead, she reached for the doorknob, turned it and let him carry her across the threshold.

Once inside, Colin kicked the door closed behind him. Then he set her on her feet and kissed her long and hard, stealing the breath from her.

Emily melted against him, her body on fire, no longer in her control. She wanted him so badly, she couldn't think straight.

She shoved his jacket over his shoulders.

He shrugged free and let it fall to the floor. His hand rose to brush the hair back from her cheek, smooth the strands down over her shoulders and grip the hem of her shirt.

Emily raised her arms, her gaze capturing his.

Ever so slowly, Colin dragged her shirt up her torso and off, tossing it to the corner of his room.

The chilly night air did nothing to cool the heat burning a path through her body and coiling at her core.

She tugged his T-shirt out of the waistband of his jeans and shoved it up his chest, eager to be done with the clothes standing between them. Her urgent need to be skin to skin drove her into a frenzy of stripping.

Clothes flew off, and soon they were naked in front of each other.

Emily's breathing was ragged as if she'd been running or she'd forgotten how to breathe in her desperate desire to be close to this man.

Colin paused to cup her face between his palms. "You're even more beautiful than you were ten years ago.

She laughed, giddy with what was happening. "You've improved on the younger model." Running her hands over his rock-hard chest, she looked up into his eyes. "I don't want to think about yesterday. Tomorrow will come whether we want it to or not. Make love to me tonight. No promises. No strings. Just us."

"What if I want promises and strings."

She touched a finger to his lips. "Don't overthink this, Marine."

He drew in a deep breath and let it out. Then he scooped her up in his arms, carried her to his bed and laid her across the quilt, lying on the bed beside her. "I've wished for a very long time to have you like this. You were what kept me alive in the desert."

"Even though I was married to Alex?" she asked.

"I knew I couldn't have you, but it was the thought of you riding like the wind on that old nag, Sassy. You laughing beside the old swimming hole, the sun making your hair look like spun gold." He lifted a strand of her hair and smiled. "You were a hope that someday I'd find someone who could put up with me." He kissed her forehead and her eyelids. "Emily, you're amazing. We should talk about this. I'm not into one-night stands."

Heart pounding, blood rushing through her veins and desire coiling tightly inside, she didn't want to think past the moment. She didn't want him to make promises in the heat of the moment. She wasn't sure what the future held for either of them. She didn't want to think that far ahead. Not when she had him naked in front of her.

She only wanted to feel.

Emily wrapped her arms around his neck and pulled him down to her mouth. "Stop talking and start moving."

"But—"

"No buts. I want you now. Don't disappoint me."

"Oh, sweetheart, there will be no disappointment." He leaned over her, parting her legs with his knee.

"That's what I wanted to hear." She sighed and leaned up to meet his lips as he positioned his body between her thighs.

For a long moment, he teased her tongue, caressing it with his own in a kiss that stole her breath away.

Then he was kissing her cheek and dragging his fingers along her jaw and down her neck, blazing a path of kisses and nibbles to the rounded swells of her breasts.

He paused there, taking one nipple between his teeth, rolling the tip against his tongue until it tightened into a hard, little bead.

Emily arched off the mattress, needing more.

He moved from that breast to the other, taking it in a similar fashion, leaving Emily breathless in his wake.

He wasn't done.

Colin slid down her body, tonguing and kissing each rib along the way, dipping into her bellybutton and slowing as he reached the mound of curls covering her sex.

By then, Emily was holding her breath, waiting for what came next. Her body teetered on the edge of something big, something colossal.

Colin parted her folds and blew a stream of air over the tightly packed bundle of nerves. Her body tingled in anticipation, ready to take whatever he would give.

And he gave.

First, he tapped a finger against the nubbin of flesh. Then he dipped that finger into her channel, swirled in her fluids and came back out to wet her clit. Slowly, he massaged that narrow strip of flesh, drenched in her own juices. As he stroked, he increased the pressure and speed.

Emily dug her heels into the mattress, holding back her moan of extreme pleasure. With her sister in the room beside Colin's, she didn't need to announce she was having sex by screaming out Colin's name. Not that she was thinking all that clearly.

Not when he was playing her like a fiddle, his fingers making music at her core.

He shifted his hand, sliding that finger and two more into her channel.

His tongue took control where his finger had been.

Sweet heaven above.

He flicked, licked and nipped at the tender flesh.

Emily reached for his head, holding him there. The joy was so intense, she wasn't sure she would survive it. But she couldn't tell him to stop. Not now. Not when she was so close...

The next flick of his tongue sent her rocketing to the stratosphere.

She let go of his hair and gripped the comforter at her sides, holding on to keep from flying to the moon.

Wave after wave of sensations washed over her, carrying her along until minutes, hours, maybe a lifetime passed, and she slowly fell back to earth.

Though her orgasm had been good, it wasn't over. She wanted more. Emily wanted him inside her, filling the empty place in her body and in her heart.

She gripped his shoulders and pulled him up her body.

When he took her mouth, she could taste her

essence on his lips and tongue. It fired up her senses and pushed her to the edge again.

Colin paused, his cock poised at her entrance, his body tense, his arms holding him above her.

"What?" she asked, breathless and ready for the next step.

"Protection," he said.

"I can't get pregnant," she said. "And I'm clean." When she'd thought Alex was cheating on her, she'd had tests run to make sure she hadn't been affected by his indiscretions.

"I am, too. But wouldn't you feel better if we had more protection?"

"I'd feel better with you inside me. Now." She gripped his ass and guided him into her channel.

He was big, his erection thick and hard.

Her orgasm had provided sufficient lubricant to ease him into her.

She pressed harder, wanting all of him.

When he'd gone as far as he could go, he stopped and waited for her body to adjust to his girth.

Impatient and needy, Emily pushed him away until he slipped nearly all the way out of her. Then she slammed him back home.

Colin took over from there, sliding in and out of her, slowly at first. Soon, he was riding her in a full gallop.

Emily held onto his hips, urging him on, loving the way he made her feel so complete.

The tingling started at her core and quickly

spread throughout her body, all the way to the very tips of her fingers. She raised her hips, meeting his thrusts with ones of her own.

The intensity of their lovemaking sent her over the edge for the second time that night.

Colin thrust one last time and remained buried deep inside her, his cock throbbing against the walls of her channel, spilling his seed inside her. He collapsed over her, his body beautifully heavy on hers.

For a moment, sadness flashed over her.

She would never bear Colin's child or any other man's child for that matter.

The thought didn't linger, not when it felt so incredibly good to be coupled with this man, his naked body lying against hers.

Just when she was feeling the need to breathe again, he rolled to his side, taking her with him.

Pulling her close, Colin rested his cheek against her hair and drew in ragged breaths. "You're amazing," he whispered against her ear.

She chuckled, a joy she hadn't felt in a very long time making her smile in the dark. "Back atcha, Marine."

"Where do we go from here?" he said softly.

"To sleep." She cupped his face in her hand and leaned forward to kiss him fully on the lips. "Sleep."

"But I want to talk."

"Talk is overrated."

He laughed. "I thought foreplay was overrated."

"Oh, no. Foreplay is way underrated. And you get an A+ for your efforts in that department." She sighed and leaned her cheek against his chest.

"What about tomorrow?" he asked.

"It'll be here before you know it," she said, refusing to get into a discussion about their future. "Everything is too complicated to sort out when I'm so sleepy, I can barely keep my eyes open."

He sighed and wrapped his arms around her. "Then sleep, sweetheart. The morning will come soon enough, and we'll have time to talk then."

Basking in the glow of the best sex she'd ever experienced, Emily drifted into sleep, lying in the arms of the man she'd always loved. Life didn't get much better than that.

A murderer was still at large, and she wasn't out of danger by any means. But for a few moments out of what had been a lousy day, she'd been happier than she could ever remember.

Too bad it wouldn't last.

CHAPTER 13

COLIN WOKE when Emily left his bed during the darkest hours of the morning.

"Where ya going?" he asked.

In the starlight streaming through the window, he could see her moving about the room, collecting clothing from the floor.

"To my room before everyone wakes up," she said.

"You think they don't already know where you spent the night?" He chuckled. "Nothing gets by my family."

"Great," Emily whispered. "I've disrespected your mother by sleeping with her son."

"She's a grown woman." He snorted. "I'm all grown up...not the teen she had to bail out of trouble all those years ago. She wouldn't have a problem with it."

"Yeah, well, I do. It's not my home. I'm a guest, and I at least need to make it look like I slept in my own bed." She slipped into her jeans and pulled her blouse over her head. With her bra and shoes in her hands, she crossed to the bed.

Colin leaned up on his elbow. "I wish you'd stay."

"If it were my own home…" She paused. "No. If it were somewhere else, I might. But not under your mother's roof." She leaned over and pressed her lips to his. "Go back to sleep."

He sat up, wrapped his arms around her and swept her off her feet.

Emily dropped the shoes and bra and rolled onto her back on the mattress beside him. "What are you doing?"

"If you won't stay, at least give me a real kiss." He took her mouth with his, starting out with a feather-soft brush of his lips across hers.

Emily captured the back of his neck and pulled him closer. Sealing her lips over his, she thrust her tongue past his teeth to tangle with his, in a dance so intimate and tempting, it left him wanting so much more than just a kiss.

His groin tightened as he slid his hand beneath her blouse and caressed her bare breast.

Emily arched her back, pressing against him. "You're making this harder."

"No…you're making *me* harder." He pinched the tip of her nipple once then rolled her out of the bed and back on her feet. "Go, before I decide to kidnap you and make you stay." He smacked her bottom with the flat of his hand and sent her toward the door.

As she walked across the room, he rose from the bed and stood naked in the starlight.

Emily paused with her hand on the doorknob and glanced back at him. "Colin…"

"Go to bed, Emily." He wanted to keep her from leaving but knew she wouldn't feel right taking advantage of his mother's hospitality. That was just the way she was, and he loved her for it. "We'll talk in the morning."

She hesitated for a moment longer then ducked out the door, closing it softly behind her.

Colin pulled on a pair of boxer shorts, staring at the door for a long time before he turned to the window.

The stars shone brightly over the Crazy Mountains that night, lighting the ground below with a soft indigo blue.

At that moment, she was probably lying down in the bed next to her sister. Was she staring out at the night like he was? Did she think about him at all? Had their lovemaking been enough to make her want to come back for more?

Staring out at the beauty of the night, he could imagine living fulltime in Montana. Especially if it meant he could be with Emily for the rest of his life.

Giving up the Marine Corps would be hard but losing Emily for the second time in his life would be harder. This time, he'd fight to win her heart, no matter what it took.

He turned away from the window and lay on the

bed. Sleep was elusive. Thoughts of making love with Emily got his heart pumping too fast and adrenaline zipping through his veins. When the gray light of pre-dawn crept over the mountains, he gave up, got up and dressed in his jeans and cowboy boots.

A good workout would help burn off the excess energy before the rest of the family started moving around.

Outside, he walked toward the barn, enjoying the brisk morning air. He didn't mind the cold. He could always dress warmer. When he'd been in the Iraqi desert, he could never seem to get cool enough.

When he opened the barn door, he thought someone had left the lights on—until he heard someone mucking straw out of a stall.

One by one, he passed stalls until he came to the one where someone was flinging soiled straw and horse manure into a wheelbarrow.

"You're up early," he said.

The person straightened and turned.

Colin laughed when he realized it was Emily. "Couldn't sleep, either?"

She smiled. "All I could think about was you standing naked in the starlight." She narrowed her eyes at him. "That wasn't a fair parting shot."

He took the pitchfork from her and leaned it against the stall wall. Then he pulled her into his arms and held her there. "What are we going to do about us?"

She sighed and leaned into him. "I don't know.

But how can you stand to hold me when I smell like horse manure?"

"I've never smelled anything nicer." He brushed straw from her hair and kissed the tip of her nose.

"I'm a recent widow. I shouldn't be fooling around with another man so soon after Alex's passing." She stood on her toes and kissed him back. "But I can't seem to help myself."

"Who said that after your spouse's death you had to grieve for the rest of your life? And who's making the rules about the length of time?" He shook his head. "If there's one thing I've learned from my time on the Marine Force Reconnaissance team, it's that life is too short to waste a single moment worrying about what others think." He kissed her again, and then just held her in his arms, loving every second her body pressed against his. "I could do this for the rest of my life."

She snorted. "Shovel horse manure?"

"Well, maybe." He leaned back and gazed into her smiling face. "But holding you would come in a close second. I like it when you smile."

Her smile faded. "I like having more reasons to smile."

"We'll find out who's giving you grief and set him straight. Then you can get on with the task of living life to the fullest." He hugged her again then set her aside. "Ready for me to dump that wheelbarrow?"

She nodded. "I thought you'd never ask."

He unloaded the wheelbarrow in the dung heap

behind the barn and returned to help her finish up the stall she'd been working on. Then they fed the horses, pigs and chickens before they returned to the house.

Yeah, he could get used to living in Montana again. He loved the feeling of a good, hard day's work and knowing the animals were well cared for and the ranch was in good shape.

Mostly, he liked the idea of coming home every evening to the woman he loved.

He had nine months left on his current enlistment. Would Emily wait around until he completed his obligation? Last night, she'd said she didn't want to talk about the future. Had she meant she didn't want to talk just last night? Or was she going to stretch it out a little longer?

He wasn't sure, but he wouldn't wait too much longer before he asked her what her plans were for the rest of her life.

His mother was cooking breakfast in the kitchen when they walked through the back door.

Angus stood at the coffee maker, pouring a cup.

"Don't drink it all," Sebastian said, as he entered the room and crossed immediately to the cabinet with the coffee mugs.

"You two ready for some breakfast?" his mother asked.

Emily smiled at her. "I'm too much of a mess to sit at the table."

"Emily and I took care of the animals," Colin explained. "We'll be down to help after we clean up."

"Lookin' tired, bro." Sebastian said as he took Angus's place at the coffeemaker and poured a cup of the fragrant brew. He turned with a grin. "Get much sleep last night?"

Emily's cheeks blossomed a bright pink.

"You do realize your bed has always had a squeaky spring in it, don't you?" Angus said.

"I'll just be going," Emily said, her face flaming.

"You boys leave your brother alone," their mother said, waving her spatula at his brothers. "You're being rude in front of our guest."

Emily gave her a weak smile and made a hasty exit out of the kitchen.

"Thanks," Colin said, his tone dripping sarcasm. "Remind me to return the favor in front of your significant others." He raised his eyebrows. "Oh, wait. Sebastian doesn't have a significant other."

"Only because I choose to play the field."

"Because no woman would put up with your bull-shit," Colin pointed out.

"Language," his mother said in her sternest voice.

"Are you telling us you have a significant other?" Angus asked, pinning Colin's gaze with a direct one of his own.

"Maybe." Colin hated to say anything until he knew for certain Emily felt the same.

His mother turned to him with a smile spreading

across her face. "Are you and Emily finally getting together?"

"Getting?" Sebastian snorted. "I'd say *got*, if the squeaky bedspring had anything to say."

Colin raised a hand, glaring at his brothers. "Don't."

"Don't what?" Sebastian gave his best wide-eyed innocent look.

"I care about Emily," Colin said. He wasn't ready to admit to his brother and mother just how much he cared. "She's been through some rough times."

"She has indeed." His mother touched his arm. "I really hope she comes around to you. I always saw her as one of us. She's family, and you two belong together. I don't know why you let Alex steal her away from you. They weren't right for each other."

He patted his mother's hand on his arm. "I'm glad you think that way. I don't know what's in our future, but I'll do my best not to screw it up this time."

She reached up and patted his face. "I just want to see you happy. And I love Emily like a daughter. I want to see her happy as well."

The telephone on the counter rang.

His mother turned to answer. "Hello." She listened, a frown forming on her brow. "Yes, of course. I'll let them know."

Before his mother completed her call, Colin's cellphone vibrated in his pocket. He pulled it out and noted the call was from Sheriff Barron. "Colin McKinnon here."

"This is Sheriff Barron. Roy Keats is conscious and wants to see you and Emily at the hospital. He said he has information that might help you find the person who paid him to torch your house. I'm headed there as soon as I check into the office."

"We'll be there in an hour."

The sheriff ended the call.

"Who was that?" his mother asked.

"Sheriff Barron. He said Roy, the guy who attacked Emily and her house, wants to see us. He's ready to talk."

"That's good news." She turned to Angus and Sebastian. "I just got off the phone with Craig Brantley, a trophy outfitter out of Bozeman. He said a couple of his hunters found a campsite on the other side of Target Rock that might be of interest to our search for your father."

The brothers straightened, their expressions serious.

"How so?" Angus asked.

"They found your father's rancher co-op card in the dust around the circle of rocks." She pressed her fingers to her lips. "He always kept that co-op card in his wallet."

"Are they going to show us where they found the campsite?" Angus asked.

She shook her head. "He's going to send you a text with the GPS coordinates and a photo of the card exactly how they found it. I gave him Angus's cellphone number."

"That's a good fifteen or twenty miles by dirt road to get back in there," Angus said, looking at his phone.

Sebastian took the phone from his mother. "I'll let Duncan know."

"We can load some horses into a trailer and take them as far as we can by road, and then ride from there."

"I'm going with you," Colin said.

Angus shook his head. "You need to go to Bozeman. Sheriff Barron will be expecting you."

"It can wait," Colin grimaced, wishing he could be in two places at one time.

"You know if you don't take Emily, she'll go without you," Sebastian said.

"He's right," their mother said. "You need to go to Bozeman. Emily needs you."

"Our father needs me, too."

"Your three brothers can check out the lead," his mother insisted.

"And I'm going with the boys." Molly entered the kitchen. Her gaze shifted from her mother to Angus and Sebastian. "What lead are we checking out?"

"We'll fill you in," Sebastian said.

"No, she needs to stay with Mom and Brenna." Angus shook his head at Sebastian. "Especially if you're coming with us."

"You're not leaving me behind," Sebastian said.

Molly crossed her arms over her chest. "Oh, right, but you can leave me behind."

Colin's mother pointed her spatula at Sebastian and Angus. "You two and Duncan will go to Target Peak." She pointed to Molly. "You'll stay to provide backup for me and Brenna. And Colin," her spatula aimed at him, "you need to go with Emily."

"Face it, Colin," Sebastian grinned. "You heard the boss."

Colin was torn. He'd come home to help find his father. His brothers would converge on the campsite and leave no stone unturned in their efforts to find their father.

Emily, on the other hand, had no one but him. And she was as important to Colin as his father. He nodded. "I'll go with Emily. But you have to promise to let me know where you are. If we get done early, we'll head your way."

"Unless you can read smoke signals, I doubt we'll be able to get word out to you," Angus said.

"Besides," Sebastian said, "it'll take us as long to get out there as it'll take you to get to Bozeman."

"You know we'll report back as soon as possible," Molly said.

Colin's gaze swept around his family. "You know I want to be there."

"We do," Angus said. "But Emily needs you, too. Go."

Colin nodded, kissed his mother's cheek and sprinted up the stairs to the bathroom.

Emily was just stepping out, wearing clean jeans and a powder blue sweater. "It's all yours," she said.

He gripped her arms, kissed her hard then stepped around her and entered the bathroom.

Emily laughed. "What was that for?"

"Because," he said and closed the door. Minutes later, he was out, wrapped in a towel, crossing the hallway to his room. He was dressed and pulling on his boots when Emily appeared in his doorway. "Ready?"

Colin nodded and straightened. "Sheriff Barron called. Roy's conscious and ready to talk."

"Good," she said. "Let's go."

Colin prayed they weren't wasting their time going all the way back to Bozeman, while his siblings could be chasing a substantial lead regarding his father's whereabouts.

CHAPTER 14

EMILY STOPPED by her bedroom and poked her head in the door once more before they left the house.

"Promise me you won't go anywhere without a backup."

Brenna held up her hand. "I promise." She frowned. "*You're* the one who needs to be careful in Bozeman. Don't let anyone run you over or push you off the road."

Emily grinned. "I'll be with Colin."

"Like you were last night?" Brenna's eyebrows lifted in challenge.

Emily's cheeks heated. "Busted."

"We're talking later," Brenna warned.

"Fine. Just be careful. I love you." Emily hurried down the stairs to where Colin waited for her at the front door.

Once in the truck, they settled in for the long drive into Bozeman. Emily sat silently, hoping Colin wouldn't bring up what had happened the night before. Everything about the night was still fresh and new. She wasn't sure what she was feeling and where they were going from there.

Colin had his career in the military.

Emily had her life in Eagle Rock. After Alex's death, she'd applied to teach at the local elementary school. She was due to start at the beginning of the next semester.

She'd quit teaching when she and Alex had decided to try to have a baby, thinking the stress was making it hard for her to get pregnant.

Now, with no baby and no husband, she knew she would have to go back to work soon. Sitting around an empty house couldn't be healthy.

"Are we going to talk about what happened?" Colin asked, breaking into Emily's thoughts.

She wrinkled her nose. "Do we have to?"

"I think we do," he said. "I don't know how much longer I'll be here. I have another two weeks of leave, and I could probably apply to extend it if we haven't found our father by then. But eventually, I have to go back to my duty station."

Emily nodded. The thought of Colin leaving made her chest tighten and her stomach knot. It was his job. He had to go.

"My enlistment is up in nine months. I've got ten years in. That's halfway to twenty and retirement."

Emily frowned. "What are you saying? Are you

telling me you're going to reenlist to finish out your twenty?"

He shook his head. "I'm saying that any more than ten years in, I might as well stay for twenty and collect retirement. Ten years is a good place to decide whether to stay or cut loose."

"What do you want to do?" Emily asked.

Colin stared at the road ahead. "I'm not going to lie to you, Emily. I love being a part of the military. My brothers in arms are just that...brothers." He glanced her way.

"But?" she prompted.

He looked back at the road. "But I've always had one regret." Colin paused, then added. "You."

"I don't want to be your regret, Colin," she said. "If you love the military, you made the right choice."

"I regret that I didn't fight for you. I bowed out when Alex asked you to marry him. You always said you'd never marry a military man. Not after watching your mother die of a broken heart."

"She died of cancer."

"And a broken heart. If she hadn't lost your father, she might have fought harder to live."

Emily nodded. "I admit, I was afraid to love a military man. I was afraid to give my heart to someone who willingly put himself in harm's way. I was wrong. I didn't realize I'd already given my heart away. It didn't become clear until after I'd married Alex." She bent her head and stared at her hands in her lap. "He knew before I did."

Colin's foot left the accelerator. "Knew what?"

"You know what."

"No," he said. "Humor me and spell it out."

She twisted her hands in her lap. "I'd given my heart to you, Colin. There. Are you happy?" She looked up at him, her eyes filled with tears. "One kiss. That's all it took, and I was head over heels. But you were my first love. I didn't know that's what it was. I'd never felt anything so profound. I was scared."

"And now?" he asked quietly.

Emily drew in a deep breath and let it out again. "I'm still scared."

He reached for her hand and held it in his, driving with the other. "I never meant to scare you, Emily."

"You didn't have to," she said with a grimace. "I'm learning that I was scared of my own feelings."

He squeezed her hand and let go, steering around a curve with both hands. "Where does that leave us?" he asked. "If you want, I can quit the military and come home to Iron Horse Ranch. But I can't quit for another eight months. I have to finish my commitment."

Emily shook her head. "I don't want you to do anything. The Marine Corps is your life."

"It has been, but it's been lonely. I don't want to lose you a second time. If it means giving up the Marines, I'll do it. Just not until my enlistment is up."

Emily smiled at him. "You'd do that for me?"

He nodded. "I would."

She shook her head. "No."

Colin frowned. "No?"

"No," she repeated. "You can't quit the military. It's part of who you are."

"I'll have to get out eventually," he reminded her.

"Until then, you need to stay the course."

"But what about what you want?" he asked.

"I admit, last night was amazing," she said.

"But?" he prompted.

"But, I'm not sure I'm ready to commit to anything. I married Alex for all the wrong reasons and made him and myself miserable." She shook her head. "I don't want to make the same mistake. I couldn't bear to make you miserable."

"I'd be happily miserable, as long as I was with you." He smiled and winked.

"You're going to be here until you find your father or two more weeks, whichever comes sooner, right?"

"I am," Colin replied.

"Give me time. I don't want to commit to anything based on great sex."

"It was pretty great, wasn't it?"

She nodded, her cheeks heating. In all the years she'd been married to Alex, their lovemaking had never been as incredibly passionate nor satisfying.

"I've been with other women, but it never felt like it did last night," Colin said. "It makes all the difference, when you're with the right person."

He was right.

And, once again, she was scared. The intensity of her feelings was such that she couldn't imagine life without Colin in it. But what if she had to face life without him in it because he was killed in battle?

Hell, Alex had proved there were no guarantees that one would live to old age. It didn't matter that he hadn't joined the military. He'd met an untimely demise in the civilian world.

Still, Emily wasn't ready to hand over her heart. The thought of saying "I love you" made her head spin and her palms sweat. "I need time."

"You've got it," he said. "But know this, Emily Tremont." He paused. "I'm not giving up without a fight. No. I'm not giving up. Period."

COLIN SPENT the rest of the drive into Bozeman ruminating over everything he and Emily had said to each other.

Though she'd said she needed time, she hadn't completely nixed the idea of a future with him. It gave Colin enough hope to hang in there. If she wanted to wait, so be it. He'd wait. But not forever.

If she didn't come around soon, he'd come up with a plan of attack to make her see what a good choice he was for her.

He loved her and didn't want to live the rest of his life without her in it.

Colin parked in the visitors' parking lot at the Bozeman hospital. He helped Emily down from his truck, took her hand and led her in through the front entrance.

Sheriff Barron met them in the lobby. When he saw them coming in, he hurried forward. "I'm sorry you two came all the way for nothing."

"What do you mean?" Colin asked.

"I just spoke with Roy. He said he didn't have any more information than he'd already given."

Emily frowned. "Then why did he call us here?"

"He didn't," the sheriff said. "Or at least, he says he didn't. His girlfriend said he was in physical therapy at the time I received the call."

"But I thought you talked to him, yourself." Colin looked past the sheriff, wondering if it would be worth going up to Roy's room and checking with the man himself.

Sheriff Barron's lips pressed into a tight line. "I've already grilled him. Either he's a good liar and I'm a bad judge of character, or the man's telling the truth."

"Who else would have made that call?"

"I don't know, but I don't see any reason for us to linger here. I need to get back to Eagle Rock." The sheriff looked from Emily to Colin. "What are your plans?"

"I guess we're headed back as well," Colin said.

"Good. I smell a setup," the sheriff said. "We can caravan back to give Emily the protection she needs."

They left the hospital together and split up in the parking lot. The sheriff headed for his service vehicle, Colin, with Emily, aimed for his truck.

Once inside, Emily sat back in her seat, frowning

heavily. "I don't understand. Who would call and say Roy was ready to talk?"

"I don't know, but let's get back to Eagle Rock. I want to know what's going on with my brothers."

"Right. You could join their search, if they're still up in the mountains." Emily's pursed her lips. "I'm sorry. You could have been out there finding your father."

"And someone could have tried to lure you to Bozeman, expecting you to come alone. I needed to be with you."

"I could have come alone," she gave him a twisted grin. "Except I don't have a car."

They didn't rehash their earlier discussion, avoiding the topic all the way back to Eagle Rock.

By the time they arrived in the small town, it was past noon.

"Do you want to stop for lunch at the diner?"

Emily shook her head. "I'd rather get back out to the ranch and make sure your mother, Molly and Brenna are okay."

He shot a glance her way. "You know you could just call them."

She smiled. "You're right. I just like to see with my own eyes, but you're right, a call would work just as well." Emily pulled her cellphone out of her purse and dialed Brenna's cellphone number.

After five rings, it rolled over to Brenna's voice mail.

Emil frowned down at the phone. "No answer."

"If she's not linked into the internet at the house, she might not be getting a signal," Colin said. "Call the landline."

Emily dialed his mother's home phone.

It rang several times before his mother finally answered. "Hello."

"Mrs. McKinnon, it's Emily. Could I speak with Brenna?"

"I'm sorry, Emily, but she's not here. She left about an hour ago to show a property to a client."

Emily's hand tightened around her cellphone. "But Sebastian went with the others."

"Oh, she didn't go alone," Mrs. McKinnon said. "Molly went as her backup."

"Okay," Emily said, although her gut was beginning to knot.

"Are you two headed out here?" Colin's mother asked. "I just pulled a roast out of the oven. We can cut it up for sandwiches."

"Yes, we're in Eagle Rock now. We'll be out there shortly." Emily ended the call and sat for a moment, wondering if she should be worried. She dialed Molly's cellphone number and waited.

After the fifth ring, Molly answered. "This is Molly." The connection was staticky, and Molly's words were hard to hear, but she didn't sound at all strange.

"How's it going?" Emily asked.

"Brenna just showed the first property. We're on our way to the second," Molly reported. "She's pretty good at this. Knows her stuff. She's actually making me consider a career in real estate."

Emily chuckled. "She loves the work. I'm sure she'd help you learn the trade, if you really want to. When do you think you'll be back?"

"Another hour, maybe?" Molly answered. "Do you need us to pick up anything from the grocery store?"

Emily smiled into the phone. "No, thanks. I'll see you two when you get here." She ended the call.

"Are they all right?" Colin asked.

"Sounds like it. They're moving on to the next property. Hopefully, they'll be back at the ranch in an hour or so."

He paused at a stop sign. "Do they need me to ride along?"

"Molly didn't say anything about needing help. In fact, my sister might just recruit her to join her real estate team."

Colin shook his head. "I can't picture Molly doing anything but ranching. You can take the girl off the ranch, but you can't take the ranch out of the girl. Or something like that." He turned the truck onto the highway, heading toward Iron Horse Ranch.

"Since the girls seem fine, you wanna reconsider and do lunch at the diner?" he asked, his eyebrows cocked hopefully.

"Your mother said she just pulled a roast out of the oven and offered it up for sandwiches," Emily reported.

Colin stepped on the accelerator. "Never mind.

Mom's roast beats anything we could get at the diner." He made the rest of the journey in silence.

If Emily wasn't mistaken, the man was practically salivating in anticipation of his mother's roast.

When they arrived at the house, Mrs. McKinnon came out of the house, a frown furrowing her brow. "I just got a call from the sheriff's office. A forest ranger relayed that your brothers are in trouble up in the mountains. Something to do with a vehicle breakdown. They need you to take your truck up there and bring the trailer and horses down."

"I'll go with you," Emily said.

Colin shook his head. "Much as I'd like that, you need to stay and wait for Molly and Brenna to get back. I'll take our foreman, Parker, with me."

Mrs. McKinnon nodded. "He wanted to head out immediately, but I told him you were coming and that he should wait and go with you."

Colin pulled Emily into his arms and kissed her soundly in front of his mother. When he stepped back, he gave his mother a pointed look. "Yes, I just kissed Emily. And no, nothing is settled between us." He grinned and spun on his heels, heading back to his truck. "Don't go anywhere," he called out.

Emily's heart was full to overflowing. She loved Colin so much, she couldn't imagine another day without him in her life.

His mother slipped her arm around Emily's waist. "You love him, don't you?"

Emily sighed. "Is it that obvious?"

"Yup," Mrs. McKinnon responded. "How long have you known?"

"Since he first kissed me ten years ago…?" Emily admitted.

His mother leaned back, her brow furrowing. "Why did you marry Alex?"

"I was young and scared," Emily said.

"Scared of what?"

"Loving someone so much that, if I lost him, I couldn't go on living."

Mrs. McKinnon's eyes filled with tears. "I know how that feels."

Emily hugged the other woman.

Colin's mother brushed a tear from her cheek. "And now?"

"Now, I know there are no guarantees in life and death. You never know how long you have on this earth."

"True," Mrs. McKinnon said. "And you have to grab for all the happiness and good memories that you can."

"And if bad things happen, you'll have no regrets because you've lived and loved as hard as you could while you could." Emily shook her head. "I told Colin I needed time to decide what I wanted to do with my life." She smiled. "I don't need any more time."

"No?" Mrs. McKinnon smiled through tear-washed eyes.

"No. I want Colin in my life, for the rest of my life and his, however long that might be." Emily stared at where the truck had disappeared down the highway and laughed. "Now that I know what I want for sure, I can't wait to tell Colin."

"And he won't be back for several hours." Mrs. McKinnon hugged her close. "I really hope this means I'm getting another daughter. As a woman who has been outnumbered by men for most of her life, I'm ready for a little more equality in the numbers." She winked. "Let's go have roast beef sandwiches for lunch. Molly and Brenna should be back soon."

CHAPTER 15

COLIN AND PARKER followed the dirt roads leading back into the Crazy Mountains that would get them close to the GPS coordinates the outfitter had given. As they neared the spot, Colin could see Angus's pickup and the horse trailer parked on the edge of the road.

Angus, Duncan and Sebastian were loading the horses into the trailer when Colin came to a stop behind them.

"Hey, Colin, couldn't stand it? You had to come see for yourself?" Sebastian asked as he tied his horse's lead on the inside of the trailer and stepped out of the way of his brothers. "We combed the area and didn't find anything else of value. If our father was here, it wasn't too long ago, but we have no way of knowing where they went from here."

Disappointment pinched Colin's stomach.

"We did see where there had been a tent pitched

and staked to the ground," Duncan said. "What's this I hear about you and Emily rocking the bedsprings last night?"

Colin glared at Sebastian and deflected the conversation into another direction "Why are you loading the horses before we hitch the trailer to my truck?"

Angus emerged from the trailer after tying his horse inside. He closed the gate and hooked his thumbs through his beltloops. "What do you mean? Why would we need to hitch the trailer to your truck?"

"Mom got word your truck was broken down, and we needed to take a truck here to haul you and the horses back to the ranch." Colin frowned. "You didn't sent word through a forest ranger?"

Angus shook his head. "My truck is working fine."

Colin's heart sank to his knees. He spun and ran back to his truck.

"What's wrong?" Angus called out.

"I'm not sure, but I think we were set up." He yanked open the door to his truck and stepped up on the running board. "I might need you back to the ranch as soon as possible."

"You really think someone was playing you?" Sebastian asked.

"Why else would they send me on a wild goose chase unless they wanted to get to Emily without us interfering. 'Bastian, if you get any kind of cellphone signal, call the ranch and warn them. I'll try the closer I get to town." He dove into the truck, cranked the engine and made a U-turn in the middle of the deserted road.

He raced along the dirt roads. At several sharp corners, he didn't slow enough and the truck bed, as empty and light as it was, swung sideways for several yards before regaining traction and straightening. Forced to slow on the treacherous roads, he worked his way down the mountain, his hands gripping the steering wheel so tightly his knuckles turned white.

He knew someone was in trouble. Whether it was Emily, Brenna, Molly or his mother, he wasn't sure, but his gut said it was someone he loved.

He wouldn't stop until he got to them and ripped apart anyone who dared to hurt them.

All the way out of the mountains, he kept checking his cellphone for service. When he emerged from the foothills, he glanced down at his cellphone. Finally, he had a signal. Not much of one, but maybe enough to call home.

He hit the number for his mother's house and waited. The bars indicating signal strength blinked off.

Colin cursed and slammed his palm against the steering wheel.

He couldn't get home fast enough.

As soon as he was within range of a cellphone tower, he placed a call.

"Hank here," Hank Patterson answered.

"I need you to locate Emily's GPS tracker. ASAP.

I'm on my way into Eagle Rock from the direction of the Crazy Mountains. I think she's in trouble."

AFTER EATING roast beef sandwiches with Mrs. McKinnon, Emily helped clean up the kitchen.

"Since everyone else is out and about, I'll take care of the animals," Emily offered.

"Oh, sweetie, that's not necessary," the older woman said. "I can do it."

The phone rang.

Mrs. McKinnon held up a finger. "I'll take that. It might be important."

"I'll be out in the barn," Emily said. "It's my happy place." She smiled and headed out of the house.

In the barn, she checked that the animals had fresh water, emptying and filling some of the buckets and troughs.

Her cellphone buzzed in her pocket, making her jump. She hadn't realized just how tense she was.

Pulling out her phone, she glanced at the screen. *Unknown Caller.*

Afraid it might be from someone reporting about her husband's killer, Emily answered.

"If you want to see your sister and the McKinnon girl alive, come to the junction of Highway 97 and Fire Tower Road in fifteen minutes. Come alone, or you'll never see your sister again."

"Wait—" she cried.

The call ended abruptly.

Emily stared at the device, her heart hammering so hard it hurt.

What should she do? The men were out of range of any communications devices. Only Mrs. McKinnon remained with Emily.

Come alone.

Emily didn't have a car. She had less than fifteen minutes to get to location. The intersection wasn't far from the gate to the Iron Horse Ranch. The drive in was long enough, she might not make it there on foot in the allotted time.

Emily glanced around the barn. Two four-wheelers were parked at the rear. She could take one of them. But if she started an engine, she'd alert Mrs. McKinnon. She might come to see what was going on and try to stop her, or worse...follow her.

Emily opted to ride a horse.

She led a dark mare out of her stall and quickly saddled her. She slipped a bridle over her head and led her out into the barnyard.

Quickly, to avoid being seen by Mrs. McKinnon, she led the horse through the front pasture gate.

Placing her foot in the stirrup, she swung up into the saddle and nudged the horse into a gallop, heading for the front of the Iron Horse Ranch.

As she neared the fence, the horse slowed to a bone-jarring trot, dancing nervously to the right.

Emily kept her hands tight on the reins, guiding the horse along the fence line toward the road junction indicated for the rendezvous. When she was within several yards of the location, she dismounted, looped the reins over the animal's neck, turned it around and swatted her backside.

The mare took off for the barn.

Emily trod softly through the grass, glancing down at her watch. She fingered the necklace she'd thought to wear that morning and prayed whoever had Molly and Brenna wouldn't make her remove it. She tucked it beneath her shirt and hurried forward with only two minutes to spare.

She crossed over the fence, careful not to get hung on the barbed wire. Emily's heart raced. She could see the road junction through a gap in the trees.

Moving shadow to shadow, she slipped through the woods until she was within twenty yards of her destination.

She drew in a breath and let it out, hoping to steady her nerves.

"I'm here," she called out.

"Emily," Brenna called out. "Be careful, he's got a gun."

"A gun that's aimed at your sister's head," the man called out.

"Don't shoot," Emily said. She raised her hands and stepped out into the open, her feet braced for flight, should she get a break.

"Come closer," the voice said.

"Show me the women," Emily demanded.

Brenna and Molly were shoved out of the

shadows and into the path. Their hands were zip-tied behind their backs, and they had streaks lining their faces where tears had made mud of the dust on their cheeks.

Emily swallowed a sob.

"I'll make a trade with you," Emily said. "Release the two women, and you take me as your hostage."

"Why makes you think you're not already my hostage?" the man asked.

She leaned to the left and right, but she couldn't see him. He had to be hiding in the shadows.

"Let them go, and I'll go with you willingly," Emily called out.

"Don't do it, Emily," Brenna cried. "I'll figure a way out of this."

"You have until the count of three to come forward, or I start shooting them," the man's voice called out."

"I'm coming," Emily said. If he took all three of them hostage, they had a better chance of overcoming him. And armed with the GPS tracking device, she stood a good chance of Colin and his friend Hank finding them.

"If it's information you want, I won't tell you anything if you hurt either one of them," Emily said as she emerged into the open.

"Maybe I just want you dead." The man stepped out of the shadows, wearing a mask over his eyes and nose.

He had a strong chin, olive-toned skin and the haze of a five-o'clock shadow darkening his chin.

"You have me now," Emily said, walking toward him with her hands in the air. "Let them go."

"I have the gun," he grumbled. "I call the shots." He motioned for her to stop. "Get down on your knees and put your hands behind your back."

A van stood to the man's left, half-hidden in the brush, with a sliding door opened wide.

Emily knew once in the van, she didn't have much of a chance to get away. Still, he was one man against the three women. Though Molly and Brenna had their hands zip-tied behind their backs, their legs were free. They could run.

Scenarios ran through Emily's mind as she knelt in front of the man and placed her hands behind her back.

He threw a plastic zip-tie at Brenna's feet. "Secure her wrists."

Brenna spit at the man. "I'm all tied up. Do it yourself."

The man fired the gun. The bullet hit the ground two feet in front of Brenna.

She jerked backward, her eyes wide. "Bastard!"

Emily held her breath until she was certain neither Brenna nor Molly had been hit. She let the air out of her lungs and urged Brenna, "Do what he said."

Brenna turned to pick up the plastic tie with her hands cinched behind her back. Then she crawled across the ground to where Emily knelt, holding her wrists behind her back.

Emily held her hands as far apart as she could, without appearing too obvious. Brenna struggled, but managed to apply the zip-tie. It appeared tight but was very loose when Emily relaxed her hands.

"In the van," their captor said. "And don't try anything funny. I'd just as soon shoot your sister as look at her."

"What do you want from us?"

"I want what's mine," he said. "Get in the van."

Emily struggled to stand and waited while Brenna leaned against her in order for them both to rise to their feet.

Molly straightened and looked from Emily to Brenna.

A plan formed in Emily's mind. If she could get them to move toward the van, they could use the van for cover and run into the woods.

As Brenna passed Emily, she whispered, "Be ready to run,"

"All of us?" she murmured.

"Yes."

"Be careful," Brenna said.

"Shut up and get in!" their captor shouted.

While Brenna and Molly were moving toward the van, Emily inched forward until she was close to the man holding the gun.

Once Brenna and Molly were past her and close enough to the van to take cover, she made her move, diving toward the man, slamming into the hand holding the gun. He fell to the ground, the gun falling free of his grip and sliding across a bed of dried leaves before coming to a halt a few feet away.

Emily landed on top of him. She pulled her hands free of the bindings and scrambled across the man, reaching for the gun. If she could get to it first, they had a chance.

An arm encircled her waist and flung her away from the weapon.

Emily rolled to her feet and glanced behind her at the man with the mask.

Brenna and Molly stood frozen to the spot in front of the open van door.

"Run," Emily screamed.

"Not without you," Brenna answered.

"I'll be okay. Just run!" Emily begged.

Instead of running away, Brenna ran toward her sister.

"No," Emily cried.

The man scrambled across the ground, grabbed the gun and rolled onto his back, pointing the weapon up at Emily. "Move, and I shoot."

Emily stared down the barrel of the pistol and knew she'd lost her chance. If Brenna and Molly hadn't run, her effort to do the right thing would have been wasted.

"Now, get int the van. All of you." He rose to his feet, holding the pistol steady.

Emily turned to find her sister and Molly had

indeed left. Her heart soared. She could endure anything, knowing her sister would be all right.

"That's right. Stay away if you don't care whether or not your sister dies," he called out.

"We care," Brenna's voice sounded from the other side of the van. She emerged into the open, hands in the air.

"Then let's do it once and get it right this time," he said. "Get into the van."

Brenna and Molly stepped up into the van.

Emily crossed the clearing and was in the process of raising a foot to get into the van when a voice gave her pause.

"Put down your gun and step away from the van."

All the air whooshed out of Emily's lungs. She recognized that voice. Her heart swelled with love and relief. Setting her foot back on the ground, she turned to find Colin standing in the sunlight, like an avenging Viking, coming to claim his lady.

"Go ahead," the man in the mask taunted. "Shoot. But you'd better do it before I pull the trigger on your girlfriend.

A shot rang out.

The man in the mask staggered backward, clutching at his chest. He fell to his knees and toppled over onto his face then laid still.

As Colin moved forward to take Emily into his arms, more men appeared, rising out of the underbrush, like ghosts coming to life.

Hank Patterson was one of the men. He knelt

beside the man on the ground, turned him over onto his back and pushed the mask off his face. Then he pressed two fingers to the base of his throat, feeling for signs of life. "He's alive."

"Who is he?" Emily asked.

Swede joined Hank, standing in front of the man on the ground. "He's Silas Hunt." Swede reached into Hunt's pocket and pulled out his cellphone. "His was one of the numbers listed on Alex Tremont's secret phone. Known for his connections to the mafia, he's considered dangerous and doesn't play nicely with others. I bet if they do a ballistics match on his gun and the bullet they found in Alex's vehicle, it'll match."

"That bastard..." Silas Hunt coughed, his lungs rattling with the effort. "He stole more than a hundred thousand dollars from me. I needed that money. It isn't mine."

"Guess your luck has run out," Sheriff Barron said, as he approached from the direction of the highway. "You won't get to spend that money where you're going."

"I should have killed the bitch myself," Silas muttered. "Keats botched the job at every attempt and didn't have the decency to die when he was shot."

The wail of a siren sounded in the distance.

An ambulance arrived. The emergency medical technicians loaded Silas Hunt into the back and carried him away to the hospital in Bozeman.

Sheriff Barron followed to make sure Hunt made

it there and wasn't waylaid along the way by his own people or the folks he owed money.

Hank and Swede cut the zip-ties off Brenna and Molly's wrists and loaded them into Hank's truck to transport them to the Iron Horse Ranch house.

Colin slipped an arm around Emily's waist and escorted her through the trees and out onto the road. They walked a tenth of a mile until they reached the spot where he'd hidden his truck and walked in on foot to stop Silas from shooting Emily.

"How did you know I was in trouble?"

"Silas must have been monitoring the law enforcement radios and knew when my brothers had gone out to investigate the campfire. He called my mother with a false report that my brothers' vehicle had broken down and they needed me to bring my truck to transport the horse trailer back to the ranch." Colin stopped beside the passenger door. "When I got out there and learned they didn't need my truck, I knew something was wrong and hurried back to town."

"Did you find me because of this?" She held up the necklace Hank had given her with the GPS tracking device.

He nodded. "Hank was the first person I called when I got in phone range. He guided me to this spot while he and his team were headed in the same direction. We just happened to converge on the location at the same time."

"Remind me to thank Hank and his team." She stared up at Colin. "And, Colin…"

"Yes, dear," he said, circling the back of her neck with his hand.

"I love you and don't want to go another day without you in it or another minute without telling you how I feel." She let out a relieved breath. "There. I said it. And I don't need any more time to think about where I want to be in the future. I want to be with you. If that's following you around from post to post, I'm game. As long as I get to see you occasionally, I'll be happy. And when you retire from the Marine Corps, I'd like to come back to my home in Montana."

He swept her up in his arms and kissed her until she was lightheaded from lack of air.

"Those are the sweetest words I've ever heard. I love you, Emily. And I promise to love and protect you for the rest of your life." He set her on her feet and dropped to one knee. "This might not be the best time or place, and I don't have the ring you deserve, but I want to get this out before you change your mind…" He took her hand in his. "Emily, will you marry me?"

She laughed and dropped down to her knees in front of him. "Yes, Colin. And I'm not going to change my mind. I love you to the stars and back."

EPILOGUE

COLIN STOOD in the living room of the Iron Horse ranch house with Emily curled into the crook of his arm, feeling better than he'd felt in a very long time.

His family had gathered to share the evening meal.

Angus's fiancée, Bree Lansing, sat on the couch beside him. They'd invited her widowed mother to come to dinner as well. She stood by Colin's mother, talking recipes and animal husbandry.

Duncan and his fiancée Fiona sat on the floor, playing with their baby Caity. Molly played peek-a-boo along with them. Caity giggled and swung her chubby fist at Molly, making her laugh.

Sebastian stood with Parker Bailey, Iron Horse Ranch's foreman, talking about the fences that needed mending the next day.

The only person missing was their father, James McKinnon, which saddened Colin's heart.

But he couldn't be completely despondent. Not now. "Emily and I have an announcement to make," he said in a clear, loud voice.

"Let me guess," Sebastian said. "She's completely lost her mind and agreed to marry your sorry ass."

Colin frowned at his brother. But the frown couldn't stay in place. He was too happy to be cranky with his brother. "You got that right. I asked, she said yes and as soon as we find Dad, we're getting married."

His mother clasped her hands together. "Thank God."

Everyone in the room laughed and swarmed around him and Emily, congratulating them.

"What? No ring?" Sebastian held up Emily's left hand, bare of any jewelry. "What kind of proposal is that?"

Emily beamed up at Colin. "The best."

He kissed her and held her close for a long moment. "We need to get this ball rolling. Dad's been gone long enough."

"Too long," Molly concurred.

"What do we have so far?" Duncan asked the room full of people.

"A ring Roy stole off Silas Hunt and a co-op card that had been in Dad's wallet when he disappeared."

"I get the feeling he's leaving breadcrumbs for us to follow," their mother said, her brow furrowed. "We just need to follow them."

A knock sounded on the front door.

"That must be Hank Patterson. He said he had some news and wanted to deliver it in person," Colin had let the man through the gate minutes earlier.

His mother hurried to the door to let the man in. He was followed by his computer guru, Swede.

He glanced around the room with a smile. "I'm sorry, am I interrupting a family reunion?"

"Not at all," Colin's mother said.

Hank turned to the man bringing up the rear behind Swede. "I ran into Sheriff Barron at the gate and thought you wouldn't mind if I let him in behind us."

"Please. Come in," Mrs. McKinnon said, waving the three gentlemen into the rapidly filling living area. "We were just going over what we had in our search for my husband. Please tell me you have something to add."

"As a matter of fact," Hank said. "We do."

"And so do I," the sheriff said. "I have more news from Silas Hunt."

The family gathered around, all anxious to hear what they had to say.

Hank nodded toward the sheriff. "You go first."

"Silas confessed to hiring thugs like Roy Keats to try to run Emily off the road and torch her house. He was also the one who ransacked it searching for the money Alex embezzled from his accounts. But he swears he had nothing to do with the explosion in the vault at the bank that destroyed Alex's safe deposit box and the ledger he had stored there."

"What about my father's ring? Did Silas own up to where he got that?"

The sheriff nodded. "He said one of his minions showed up one day wearing it. He suspected the man was working another mercenary gig on the side. He took the ring from him and then fired him. He kept the ring in his pocket, knowing that if he was caught with it, he'd be accused of kidnapping or murder."

"Did he ask his minion where he got it?"

"Silas said the guy refused to say and get anyone else in trouble."

"Who was his minion? We need to question him," Angus said.

"Not going to do any good," the sheriff said. "Remember that clip a week or so ago on the evening news about a motorcycle rider getting hit by a tractor trailer rig?"

"That was him?" Bree asked.

The sheriff nodded. "Died instantly."

"Convenient," Sebastian muttered.

Emily frowned. "If Silas wasn't responsible for the explosion, who was?"

"We don't have an answer for that, but we might have a starting point," Swede said. He looked to the sheriff. "May I?"

The sheriff waved a hand, giving him the floor.

Swede held up Alex's secret cellphone. "I hacked into this phone number's records and tracked down as many of the numbers called by this one. I found several to Silas Hunt or associates of his. One was an international number to a bank in the Cayman Islands." He grinned. "Naturally, I strolled through the bank's database and came up with an account under Alex Tremont's accounting firm. The man had a lot of money set aside for a rainy day." He smiled at Emily. "You'll be happy to know, he put your name on the account. The money is yours. All you have to do is get in touch with the bank and claim it."

"Just how much is there?" Emily asked.

"Over a million dollars," Swede sad. "Some of the transfers came from accounts belonging to Silas Hunt. Others were from legitimate businesses. But there was an account for a corporation. I tried to poke around in the corporation's records to see if I could find out who owns it." Swede's lips twisted. "I'm not saying I can't get through the security fire-wall. But I am saying I can't get through...yet. We're wondering if another one of Alex's dirty customers is afraid his information will get out and that's why they destroyed the vault at the bank in Bozeman."

"What would that have to do with our father?" Molly asked.

"The convict escaped to find the money he stole. Silas came looking for the money Alex stole from him," Hank said. "Who's to say Alex didn't work with other unsavory characters who are now desperate to keep their secrets safe?"

"Looks like we have more work to do here." Angus faced Hank. "Can we continue to count on you and your Brotherhood Protectors to help with the technical work?"

"You bet," Hank said. "And if you should need any of my guys for anything else, just give me a shout. We're here to help. And if any of you plan on getting out of the military and are looking for a civilian occupation...come talk to me. I can always use more good men." With that parting comment, Hank and Swede left the house.

With dinner over and the exciting news shared, family members left to go to their respective bedrooms or homes in town.

Colin took Emily's hand and walked with her up the stairs. "Will you be moving in with me?"

She snorted. "No. We're not married. And though your mother would be fine with it, now that we're engaged, I still feel like I should sleep in the room next to yours."

"Okay."

Emily frowned. "You're giving up already?"

He lifted his shoulder and let it drop. "You make a good point. And you've agreed to marry me. I can wait for you to move in with me until after we take our vows." He gripped her around the waist and spun her to face him. "As long as you agree to a speedy wedding." Then he kissed her long and hard, caressing her tongue in a slow, sensuous slide.

"I said I wouldn't move in with you until we were married. I didn't say sex was out of the question."

Colin's eyes widened with his grin. "In that

case…" he took her hand and led her toward the stairs.

She planted her feet, bringing them both to an abrupt halt at the base of the staircase. With a sassy gleam in her eyes, she gave him a sly grin. "First one to the top, gets to be on top."

Colin took the steps two at a time, slowing the closer he got to the landing above.

Emily reached it first. "Hey, you let me win."

"Damn right I did. I'm all about letting women be on the top. Now, I can't wait to collect my prize."

"There aren't any prizes," she said with a chuckle.

"*Au contraire*, my sweet Emily. I'm the luckiest man alive. I won the lottery when you agreed to marry me."

"That makes us both winners," she said and stood on her toes to plant a kiss on his lips. "Now, quit stallin', I won that race up the stairs, and I'm collecting on my prize." She took his hand and led him into his bedroom where they made love late into the night, rocking the squeaky spring until they both vowed to shoot it the next morning.

MONTANA SEAL

BROTHERHOOD PROTECTORS SERIES
BOOK #1

New York Times & USA Today
Bestselling Author

ELLE JAMES

New York Times & USA Today Bestselling Author

ELLE JAMES

MONTANA
SEAL

BROTHERHOOD PROTECTORS

CHAPTER 1

"MONTANA, TAKE POINT," Big Bird said. "You'll need to move in fast, once I take out the guard."

Henry "Hank" Patterson, aka Montana, adjusted his night vision goggles, gripped his M4A1 rifle with the SOP Mod upgrade and rose from his concealed position on the edge of the Iraqi village. U.S. Army intelligence guys had it from a trusted source that an influential leader of the ISIS movement had set up shop in the former home of the now dead Sheik Ghazi Sattar, a paramount chief of the Rishawi tribe. The once palatial estate had taken mortar fire from the Islamic State of Iraq and Syria—or ISIS—rebels. The sheik and his fighters had succumbed to the overpowering forces and died in battle.

In the process, ISIS had gained a stronghold in the village and captured an aid worker the U.S. government wanted returned. When ISIS offered the aid worker in exchange for captured members of their party, the current administration held to its stand that it didn't negotiate with terrorists.

That's where the navy SEALs came in. Under the cover of night, armed with limited intel and specialized sound-suppressed weapons, SEAL Team 10 was to infiltrate the compound, kill the leader, Abu Sayyaf, and liberate the aid worker, who happened to be the Secretary of Defense's niece.

Piece of cake, Montana assured himself. This was what he lived for. Or at least he'd been telling himself that for the past year. He was coming up on the anniversary of his enlistment, and he had to decide whether to get out of the military or re-up. Reenlistment meant more wear and tear on his body and more chances of being shot, blown up or bored out of his mind. When they were called to duty, the missions were intense, yet the downtime gave him too much time to think.

Besides, he wasn't getting any younger. If he didn't leave active duty, he'd end up training SEALs, rather than conducting missions. That would give him even more time to think about what could have been back in his home state.

How many years had it been since he'd visited home? Eight? Ten? Hell, it had been eleven years since he'd been back to Montana. He could remember that defining night like it was yesterday. He'd just broken up with Sadie. He was hurting and wondering if they were insane to give up the best thing that had ever happened to them. Then he and his father had a big blow out. His father called him a lazy, good-for-nothing son and told him to get to work or get out.

Looking back, breaking up with Sadie had been the best thing, all the way around. She'd gone on to become a Hollywood mega-star, and Montana had gotten the hell away from his father, joined the Navy and become a member of an elite force. Life had turned out pretty good for them both.

So why did he still think about home...and Sadie? Hell, he knew why. Every time his reenlistment came up, he started thinking about home. Most of his friends from high school were married and had children. He'd always wanted kids, but SEALs made crummy parents and spouses. They were gone most of the time, sometimes without a way to contact loved ones back home.

"Be ready." Lieutenant Mike lay next to Montana. "Big Bird, hold your fire until I give the cue."

"Roger," Big Bird responded.

New to the team, Lt. Mike wasn't new to being a SEAL. With four years and ten deployments under his belt, he was a seasoned warrior, although his recent marriage seemed to have slowed him down. He wasn't as quick to leap into a bad situation. And if rumor had it right, his wife was expecting their first child.

"Let's do it," Lt. Mike said.

The muted thump of Big Bird's rifle discharging was Montana's signal to take off.

The ISIS guard who had been pacing the top of a roof slumped forward and fell to the ground with a soft whomp.

Montana held his breath, straining his ears for the shout of alarm that didn't come. With the sentry eliminated, Montana had a clear path to the wall. He took off running, hunkered low, his weapon ready, his gaze scanning the top of the wall, searching for the tell-tale green heat signature of a warm body through his night vision goggles.

Swede and Stingray were right behind him.

His skin crawled and his gut clenched. Something didn't feel right. But the mission had to move forward. They had an enemy target to acquire and a woman to rescue before they could go home to Virginia.

Montana knelt at the base of the wall, slung his rifle over his arm, cupped his hands and bent low.

Swede ran up to him, stepped into his cupped hands and launched himself into the air. He hooked his arms over the top, dragged himself over and dropped to the ground below.

Stingray came next, then Nacho, Irish and Lt. Mike.

Big Bird would remain on top of a nearby building and be their eyes and ears for anyone approaching the compound. He'd also provide cover fire for them as they exited with the aid worker.

Lieutenant Mike, the newest member of the team,

paused at the top of the wall and reached a hand down to Montana, pulling him up and over.

Swede and Nacho had already moved forward to the main building, one side of which was caved in, like an open wound. The remaining walls bore pock-marks from bullets and shrapnel. The huge wooden door still stood, closed and strangely unguarded.

"It doesn't feel right," Swede whispered into Montana's headset.

"Stay the course," Lt. Mike responded.

"Going in," Swede acknowledged and slipped into the broken corner of the structure, climbing over the half-wall still standing.

Nacho waited a moment until Swede said, "Clear."

Nacho hopped over the wall and through the crumbled bricks, disappearing into the gaping hole.

Lt. Mike went next, then Montana. Irish brought up the rear.

Once inside, what walls still stood seemed to close in on Montana.

Lt. Mike forged ahead, hurrying past the crumbled bricks and mortar.

Swede and Nacho stood at a door leading deeper into the once ornate residence. Swede wedged a knife into the doorjamb, while Nacho aimed his rifle at the door, ready for anything. A quick jab and the lock gave. Swede nodded to Nacho, yanked open the door and stood back. Nothing happened. Nacho dove through the opening and to the side, leaving room for Swede to follow. Lt. Mike entered next.

The team moved through the building, room by room.

"There's nobody here," Montana said.

"Then why the guard on top of the building?" Big Bird asked, still connected via the two-way radios in their helmets.

"Suppose it's a trap?" Irish asked.

"We have to check all rooms." Lt. Mike said.

Montana fought a groan. The place had to be over twelve thousand square feet. And that didn't include any underground bunkers that might be a part of the former Sheik's defense plan. Lt. Mike was right. If they didn't check all the rooms, they couldn't say with one hundred percent certainty their ISIS target and the captured aid worker were not there.

Once they'd completed checking the ground floor and upper levels, they started down a set of stairs. These steps weren't finished in the opulent granite tiles of the main level. They were plain concrete, leading to a steel door, heavily reinforced.

Montana took the lead again, fixed C-4 explosives near the handle and pushed a detonator into the clay-like substance.

Everyone backed up the stairs to the main level and held their hands over their ears.

Montana pressed the detonation button. A dull thump shook the floor beneath his feet. A cloud of dust puffed up the staircase.

Lt. Mike held up a hand. "Let it clear a little."

Finally, he lowered his hand and led the way back down the stairs to the door.

It hung open on its hinges, a dark, ragged hole blown through the metal. The entrance led to a tunnel-like hallway with doors on either side. Yellowed, florescent lights flickered in the ceiling. Another door marked the end of the long hallway.

The team split, each clearing the rooms, one at a time. None were locked, but the locking mechanisms were on the outsides of the doors. A chill slithered down the back of Montana's neck, partly because of the coolness in the basement and partly from knowing the sheik had probably used the rooms to incarcerate people. Nothing in any of the rooms indicated the aid worker had been imprisoned there.

At the end of the corridor, the final door was locked. Once again, Montana set the charge, the team hid behind the doors of the cell-like rooms, waiting for the charge to blow. Montana only used enough explosive to dislodge the lock mechanism, no more. He didn't want to destroy the structure of the underground portion of the building and risk trapping his team or causing them injury with the concussion.

"You have a gift." Nacho grinned as he passed Montana and followed Lt. Mike into a much narrower tunnel.

"We're in a tunnel beneath the compound," Lt. Mike said into the two-way radio.

Montana doubted Big Bird would hear on the outside. Where the tunnel would lead, they'd know soon enough. Unfortunately, they wouldn't have a sniper on the other end providing cover for them when they emerged from whatever building.

His gut twisting, his nerves stretched, Montana clenched his weapon, holding it at the ready as he continued forward. If they had any chance of rescuing the aid worker, it had to be soon. ISIS rebels had a habit of torturing and killing anyone they could use as an example, rather than hanging on to them. Prisoners only slowed the attack and hampered their determination to take everything in their paths.

The tunnel opened into the bowels of what appeared to be a warehouse.

"I feel like we're on a wild goose chase," Swede muttered.

"And the goose is leading us to the slaughter. Not the other way around," Irish concurred.

They climbed a set of stairs to a huge, empty room.

"Damn," Swede said and bent to a dark lump on the ground.

Nacho released a string of profanity in Spanish.

"We've found the aid worker."

What Montana had assumed was a pile of rags, was in fact a woman, her clothes torn, her body ravaged, her face battered. Her eyes were wide open, staring up at the ceiling.

Swede knelt beside her and touched his fingers to the base of her throat.

Montana's stomach roiled at the sight of the woman's damaged body. He could have told Swede she was already dead. What a waste of life. And for what? "We need to get out of here."

The sound of footsteps made Montana glance up. A man stood on a catwalk twenty feet above them. He shouted something in Pashtu, ending in *Allah*, pulled the pin on a grenade and tossed it into the middle of the team.

"Fuck!" Montana yanked his weapon around and shot the man. He fell to the ground, but killing him was a little too late.

The grenade rolled toward Swede, still crouched beside the woman's body.

"Get down!" Lt. Mike shouted, and then threw himself over the grenade.

Montana shouted, "No!" as the grenade exploded beneath their leader.

The force of the concussion reverberated throughout the room, knocking Montana to the ground. His last thoughts were of the home and the girl he'd once loved.

ABOUT THE AUTHOR

ELLE JAMES also writing as MYLA JACKSON is a *New York Times* and *USA Today* Bestselling author of books including cowboys, intrigues and paranormal adventures that keep her readers on the edges of their seats. When she's not at her computer, she's traveling, snow skiing, boating, or riding her ATV, dreaming up new stories. Learn more about Elle James at www.ellejames.com

Website | Facebook | Twitter | GoodReads | Newsletter | BookBub | Amazon

Or visit her alter ego Myla Jackson at mylajackson.com
Website | Facebook | Twitter | Newsletter

Follow Me!
www.ellejames.com
ellejames@ellejames.com

ALSO BY ELLE JAMES

Iron Horse Legacy

Soldier's Duty (#1)

Ranger's Baby (#2)

Marine's Promise (#3)

SEAL's Vow (#4) TBD

Brotherhood Protectors Series

Montana SEAL (#1)

Bride Protector SEAL (#2)

Montana D-Force (#3)

Cowboy D-Force (#4)

Montana Ranger (#5)

Montana Dog Soldier (#6)

Montana SEAL Daddy (#7)

Montana Ranger's Wedding Vow (#8)

Montana SEAL Undercover Daddy (#9)

Cape Cod SEAL Rescue (#10)

Montana SEAL Friendly Fire (#11)

Montana SEAL's Mail-Order Bride (#12)

SEAL Justice (#13)

Ranger Creed (#14)

Delta Force Strong (#15)

Montana Rescue (Sleeper SEAL)

Hot SEAL Salty Dog (SEALs in Paradise)

Hot SEAL Hawaiian Nights (SEALs in Paradise)

Brotherhood Protectors Vol 1

Hellfire Series

Hellfire, Texas (#1)

Justice Burning (#2)

Smoldering Desire (#3)

Hellfire in High Heels (#4)

Playing With Fire (#5)

Up in Flames (#6)

Total Meltdown (#7)

Declan's Defenders

Marine Force Recon (#1)

Show of Force (#2)

Full Force (#3)

Driving Force (#4)

Tactical Force (#5)

Disruptive Force (#6)

Mission: Six

One Intrepid SEAL

Two Dauntless Hearts

Three Courageous Words

Four Relentless Days

Five Ways to Surrender

Six Minutes to Midnight

Hearts & Heroes Series

Wyatt's War (#1)

Mack's Witness (#2)

Ronin's Return (#3)

Sam's Surrender (#4)

Take No Prisoners Series

SEAL's Honor (#1)

SEAL'S Desire (#2)

SEAL's Embrace (#3)

SEAL's Obsession (#4)

SEAL's Proposal (#5)

SEAL's Seduction (#6)

SEAL'S Defiance (#7)

SEAL's Deception (#8)

SEAL's Deliverance (#9)

SEAL's Ultimate Challenge (#10)

Texas Billionaire Club

Tarzan & Janine (#1)

Something To Talk About (#2)

Who's Your Daddy (#3)

Love & War (#4)

Ballistic Cowboy

Hot Combat (#1)

Hot Target (#2)

Hot Zone (#3)

Hot Velocity (#4)

Cajun Magic Mystery Series

Voodoo on the Bayou (#1)

Voodoo for Two (#2)

Deja Voodoo (#3)

Cajun Magic Mysteries Books 1-3

Billionaire Online Dating Service

The Billionaire Husband Test (#1)

The Billionaire Cinderella Test (#2)

The Billionaire Bride Test (#3)

The Billionaire Daddy Test (#4)

The Billionaire Matchmaker Test (#5)

SEAL Of My Own

Navy SEAL Survival

Navy SEAL Captive

Navy SEAL To Die For

Navy SEAL Six Pack

Devil's Shroud Series

Deadly Reckoning (#1)

Deadly Engagement (#2)

Deadly Liaisons (#3)

Deadly Allure (#4)

Deadly Obsession (#5)

Deadly Fall (#6)

Covert Cowboys Inc Series

Triggered (#1)

Taking Aim (#2)

Bodyguard Under Fire (#3)

Cowboy Resurrected (#4)

Navy SEAL Justice (#5)

Navy SEAL Newlywed (#6)

High Country Hideout (#7)

Clandestine Christmas (#8)

Thunder Horse Series

Hostage to Thunder Horse (#1)

Thunder Horse Heritage (#2)

Thunder Horse Redemption (#3)

Christmas at Thunder Horse Ranch (#4)

Protecting the Colton Bride

Protecting the Colton Bride & Colton's Cowboy Code

Heir to Murder

Secret Service Rescue

High Octane Heroes

Haunted

Engaged with the Boss

Cowboy Brigade

Time Raiders: The Whisper

Bundle of Trouble

Killer Body

Operation XOXO

An Unexpected Clue

Baby Bling

Under Suspicion, With Child

Texas-Size Secrets

Cowboy Sanctuary

Lakota Baby

Dakota Meltdown

Beneath the Texas Moon

Made in the USA
San Bernardino, CA
12 December 2019

61291610R00144